new chicago stories

new chicago stories

edited by
Fred L. Gardaphè

City Stoop Press
Chicago
1990

Acknowledgements

Grateful acknowledgement is made to the following:

Tony Ardizzone, "Idling": copyright 1986 by Tony Ardizzone.
Reprinted from *The Evening News*, published by University of
Georgia Press.

Paul Hoover, "Demonstration": copyright 1987 by Paul Hoover.
Reprinted from *The New Yorker*.

Thomas J. Keevers, "Thanksgiving Day in Homicide": copyright
1982 by Thomas J. Keevers. Reprinted from *The Clothesline
Review*.

Susan Lynne House, "A Tin of Tobacco Under Her Wing":
copyright 1986 by Susan Lynne House. Reprinted from *Mundelein
Review*.

Cover photograph by Scott Mutter

Cover design by Loraine Edwalds

Interior design by Midge Stocker

Typeset by MS Editorial Service, Chicago, Illinois
text in Sabon 11.5/13.5

City Stoop Press
4317 N. Wolcott
Chicago, Illinois 60613

LC 90-084015

ISBN 0-9627425-0-3

Contents

Telling Lives: An Introduction

On hot summer nights city stoops swell with folks full of stories. The open windows of hot homes funnel the voices of neighbors with stories that fill the night. Front steps, back porches and bar stools become seats for the audiences of countless storytellers; and all this is an interaction that creates imagination and adds to local knowledge. Through the neighborhoods run the streets that guide walkers and talkers to and from their neighborhoods, through the dusk, carrying stories along into the night. In the city, there's no escaping a story. In the city, stories have lives of their own. As they move from person to person, from place to place, good stories change listeners into storytellers.

I grew up in an Italian neighborhood in which good stories never died. As long as a good memory was nearby, the past could always speak to the present. In such "old" neighborhoods, the oral traditions were kept alive through the constant interaction among families and friends. Even though my father died when I was young, there was never a lack of people in my neighborhood who, over a beef sandwich, an Italian ice, or a glass of someone's homemade wine, could tell me stories that made him live again. And as long as that oral system operated, the need for reading and writing was limited.

Reading anything beyond newspapers and the mail required escaping from my family. My reading first propelled me mentally, then physically away from my neighborhood and into libraries and schools. I read for a long time before I found literature that validated my own ethnicity and cultural experience.

Ironically, all this reading led me back to my neighborhood. As I read stories by Italian Americans I found that, in spite of many differences, there were similarities which we shared with others of different cultural backgrounds. Reading stories by writers from different cultures helped me to recognize and appreciate both the differences and similarities that people bring to city life. In short, I was developing a multi-cultural perspective, a way of seeing things through others' eyes.

As the old neighborhoods dissolve through urban renewal and migration, that everyday contact with the past gives way to occasional encounters in which, at best, only a small number of stories gets passed on. When this happens, we lose our access to a past that can not only inform and enhance the present, but help shape the future as well. This loss surfaces in unanswered questions and creates an emptiness that needs to be filled.

Good writing begins with good questions; and many writers begin by filling the great voids in their lives. There is no doubt that for urban Americans the number of questions and the size of the voids are growing. It is typical of any advanced literate society to depend less and less on its elders and storytellers. After all, the past is recorded in books, in films, and on tapes; dependence on the elder's memory is exchanged for dependence on the expert.

The stories collected here represent the tale trafficking that is common to any city's life. They are the stories of coming and going that can be heard in almost any city location. For generations such travelling stories have been carried from one neighborhood to the next by strangers who, because they did write, were elected as spokespersons for life in the city, and in Chicago, these experts became the Chicago Writer.

In a published roundtable discussion of just what the Chicago writer is, Maxine Chernoff responded with, "Many of the writers you think of as the Chicago writers are the brawling, barroom kind of writers that might portray a man's point of view" (*TriQuarterly* 60, 1984: 333). What Chernoff was speaking of is the overshadowing of the voice of "the other," a voice which is certainly key to this collection, a collection which should provide evidence that there is no single type of Chicago writer. For many years, the stories of many others have remained in the shadows of the tough guy realist stereotypes of the "Chicago Writer."

This collection offers an insight into the storytellers who have not subscribed to what has been traditionally called the "Chicago School," and yet, the works here quite often resemble the realism that has come to be synonymous with Chicago writing. If there is no such thing as the definitive Chicago writer, then perhaps there still remains the Chicago story.

The stories presented in this collection tell tales of a new Chicago, a Chicago that, like the Scott Mutter montage that fronts this book, is made up of diverse images that when brought together suggest new ways of seeing, and in the process provide alternative interpretations of life in the city. Like Mutter, the writers combine various images of Chicago to give us something much more than the typical monochrome, historical still life.

Any resemblance here to "Chicago School" writing is perhaps more a result of the up-front intensity which city life forces upon its inhabitants

than to traceable literary influences. Someone loses
self-control and in the process gains control over
your destiny. A policeman takes his frustrations out
on *your* head with a billy club, a fight starts in a bar
and *your* life is threatened. There are realities of city
life that do not change from generation to
generation. And stories connected to life in the city
cannot avoid dealing with these realities.

The writers gathered here are Chicago writers in
the sense that they have experienced some portion of
their lives in Chicago, and that experience has in
some way entered into and given a sense of place to
the stories they have chosen to tell. What you will
find in this collection is a multi-cultural
neighborhood in print, a neighborhood which has
yet to surface on Chicago streets, one which is
perhaps still years away in a city that touts its
culturally plural make-up while still enforcing rigid
boundaries between segregated neighborhoods.
There is a richness and diversity in these pages that
can only come from the juxtaposition of
multi-cultural voices.

These voices, while representing a number of the
many cultures that make up Chicago, all reach
beyond the physical and psychological boundaries
typically attributed to Chicago. They speak to a
changing America, an America that has awakened
from decades of a false, prosperity-driven revelry
with a reality hangover. They speak of an America
that must now begin to turn its attention to the social
and environmental problems it has too long ignored.

Murder by industrial pollution (often masked by
self-abuse), racism, homophobia, disintegration of
family life, the struggle for control of one's own body
and mind, the troubles facing a growing elderly

population, the subjugation of minority cultures to the self-sustaining hegemony of the rich, the white, the male, are all issues confronted by the writers of these stories. Their ability to make literature that makes sense through stories that speak through a range of voices, creates a new, perhaps even an urgent, sense of Chicago realism. Their stories demonstrate a joyful, passionate commitment to a literary art that connects directly to the lives of people on the streets. This making of literature out of lives for lives can redirect and renew the lives of those who come in contact with their stories.

These storytellers are witnesses to city life, who in the process of creating their stories also create new histories. They provide testimony to a new Chicago, a Chicago that while steeped in an American tradition challenges the narrow boundaries of its perceived stereotype. But there is more to these stories than their powerful social contexts and political statements. The writers gathered here are proof of a new source of power in storytelling. The vitality of their voices and the variations in their styles demonstrate that a city known for its provincialism and political corruption does breed alternatives that can renew our urban culture.

Fred L. Gardaphè
Columbia College, Chicago

Steve Bosak

Spooner

There's good fishing up around Spooner, Wisconsin. Dancing at the Double Dice Lounge can be fun, a change of pace. But we mostly went to Spooner to keep Macklin from having a nervous breakdown. We'd go prepared: cooler full of beer and hard salami, two cartons of cigarettes, plaid shirts, wool socks, poles, lures and methedrine. We'd meet in the alley behind Macklin's flat on the north side of Chicago. I'd pull up in the pre-dawn silence in my Oldsmobile: power windows, power mirrors, a trunk big enough for me to haul around ceramic swans and hot alarm clocks for extra cash at the weekend flea markets in the suburbs.

Joe would arrive first, satchel-assed and glum from taking the bus from the Cal-Sag canal into the city. He'd rub at his red eyes and run his knuckles through his drill-instructor flattop.

The Litowski sisters would amble up next. They were Macklin's. As much Macklin's as his hide-a-bed couch, his wall full of taxidermed bass and the M-16 rifle with the lead poured down the barrel. I never gave the sisters much thought. What can you think about identical twins that neck with each other? They weren't perfectly identical though. Marie had larger breasts than Martha. But they both had the same wide, oriental-looking faces.

But as I say, they were Macklin's girls, and he swore he never 'violated the sanctity of their bodies.' That last phrase in his own words. I never heard them complain about the arrangement. Come to think of it, I've rarely heard them say much at all. So on the days that we were set for Spooner, they'd get in the back seat and hold hands until Macklin came out.

It would be the first bright light of dawn, sunlight pouring through the gangway, and Macklin would appear. He'd wear a three-piece white suit, white Oxfords, a wide brimmed Panama and a pair of silver lensed sunglasses. If he had money left from his disability check he'd be puffing on those imported Italian cigars that are black as dried turd and arthritically gnarled. You'd think he was a pimp. He'd climb into the back with the sisters—one on each side; Joe and I would get in the front. I'd head us up toward Spooner without saying much of anything, real quiet and professional like a Greyhound bus driver. I like to keep things simple.

In that early morning as we headed to the Wisconsin border Macklin would be all smiles and laughs, wholesome color in his thin face, alert and relaxed enough to resemble Steve Lawrence. But after a palm full of methedrine and slugs of whiskey from his hip flask, he would begin to turn. About the time the whiskey and meth took hold, just about the time we reached the four lane across the Illinois-Wisconsin border, he'd take on a rough, evil look. His facial skin slackened, paled: his Charles Laughton stage. When he got that way he'd make Joe light his cigars, he'd bitch about the weather, tell the Litowski sisters to take off their halter tops. You'd think any red-blooded guy wouldn't mind seeing bare-chested women in his rear view mirror. Not me. Not under those conditions. You could plainly see by the looks on the sisters' faces that they'd prefer to leave their shirts on, and after complying with Macklin's demands, their breasts looked kind of startled and lonely in the back seat. It always sent the wrong kind of shivers up my spine. Besides all this deplorable drug-induced behavior, Macklin had one ingrained eccentricity—he paid for everything. If I got a speeding ticket, he'd pay it. He shelled out for the gas, food, found the Litowski sisters a good doctor the last time their father beat them up, and even bought Joe a space heater for his shack on the Cal-Sag canal outside the city. I've heard rumors that he pays his ex-girlfriend, Joyce Moribundi, something akin to alimony, checks regular as rent, even though he was never married to her. So I guess you could say Macklin was generous. Weird generous. But when you're hawking ceramic swans for a living out of the trunk of your car you learn to accept generosity with few questions and many thanks.

That new four-laner that curves up toward Lake Superior, tall pines towering in its wide median strip, ends up as a patched, narrow county road that leads straight up to Spooner, Hayward and beyond, where God left his moccasins. It was always dinner time when we pulled into the Spooner area. We'd wolf down some Canadian bacon and cheese omelettes at a buttery-yellow diner, steel leaders and rubber worms in a case by the cash register, while Macklin stayed in the car and "divined," he'd say, where we should bunk for the night. There are dozens of small, cold lakes around Spooner, and in early autumn there are plenty of empty cabins in the Ma-and-Pa resorts. You know the kind: knot-hole pine contact paper slapped on the three-foot tall refrigerator, lumpy quilts on bunk beds, wasp nests as thick as icicles under the eaves, a note in red crayon from the management instructing you to wrap and burn all garbage. So after our omelette dinners we'd cast off for one of those frightfully cozy cottages.

We'd settle into our new digs, Macklin and the Litowski sisters always taking the largest bedroom. After all the gear was stored, we'd break out some salami for a late snack at a dimly lit formica table, and turn in early. That day would have meant twelve hours at the wheel for me, but, as I say, I'm a natural driver.

And we were all good at sleeping. Nothing but beer farts and snores came out of that cabin before one, two o'clock. Joe and me would load up a rented boat down at the pier with our rods and a fresh bucket of chubs, then go back and get Macklin and the sisters awake enough to hold poles in their hands. I took the motor, of course. The sisters, modestly clothed in plaid shirt and painter's paints, their blond hair tucked into stocking caps, usually sat in the middle. Joe squatted to the front of them, and Macklin, in his rumpled, slept-in suit, would command the bow. He picked the spots: weed beds amid shaded coves; wide open, deep blue expanses close to the shallow, sandy shore. He was always after muskellunge. Muskie. Some call the Muskellunge the freshwater barracuda. Any muskie under thirty-six inches has to be thrown back—too small by state law.

Macklin would stare out from the bow, his mirrored glasses catching the sharp afternoon sun as it reflected from the rippling water, and he'd say softly but rock-hard serious: "Muskie. There's muskie out there. I'm gettin' one this time, ya hear?" And we'd nod solemnly. There's nothing else you can do in the face of that much determination. Of course

Macklin never caught a muskellunge. Never even
had a close call. And I'm damn glad. What the hell
do you do with a three-and-a-half foot long fish once
you hook it? With teeth like sharpened baseball
spikes? In a small boat with two spooky twin Polish
women and no-count losers like Joe and myself? I
sincerely believe you have to shoot anything that gets
that big. As far as I'm concerned, a bullet is the
highest form of respect. And I respect huge muskies.
Forty-five caliber respect, which, naturally, we didn't
have. The only thing more dangerous than a hooked,
enraged muskellunge in the midst of the likes of us
would be a loaded firearm. So it's all well and fine
that Macklin never laid a hook into one of them
toothy demons. We'd all catch bass, though.
Macklin, in fact, had one whole wall of his
apartment done-up in stuffed bass: largemouth,
brownies, stripers, ten and fifteen-pounders. They
covered an entire wall. Given the time to count, I bet
there's forty, fifty fish eyes glaring down from that
living room wall.

The sisters, in reality, did not fish much. Instead
they nuzzled each other and drank beer, running
their fingers in over each others jean tops, nibbling
ear lobes: real malformed behavior. But the whole
afternoon mood would be dictated by Macklin and
muskie fishing. When it was getting obvious that all
he'd ever pull up were bass, he'd begin to curse at the
lake. A fine under-the-breath cussing that meant
business, as if only the muskie were meant to hear.

Near dusk, the red sun setting below the green
pines and glowing in the calm water of the lake like
in some beer commercial, we'd head back to the
cabin. The girls and Macklin would disappear into
their bedroom after the customary fish fry. Joe and

me would play poker, barely speaking a word. I'd
hear a coo of passion coming from the bedroom
from time to time, but mostly the kitchen was quiet
except for the shuffling of cards and the sudden snap
and gush of our beer cans. On other nights we'd all
pile into my Olds and go to the Double Dice Lounge
outside of Hayward on Stone Lake.

Frank Talbot, a skinny old Indian with black eyes
and a splatter of pockmarks across his chin and jaw
from a load of buckshot he walked in front of,
owned what might be called a lounge. Actually the
Double Dice was a cinder brick roadhouse with
carpet remnants on the floor and a tattered acoustic
ceiling. Frank kept pickled eggs and bass in cream
sauce behind the bar just below the last row of
bottles and had a jukebox and a pool table that was
missing the eight ball—some jerk walked off with it
one night. Macklin would buy all the drinks. Drinks
for the whole bar: red-wigged Grace Heller who runs
the Stone Lake Exxon, Dan Mustlamb, a simpleton
in bright red double-knit pants so no one'd run him
down when he walked the dark two-laner home, a
drunk Indian girl with chapped lips and some
cigarette ashes caught in her long hair, two guys who
would sit at the end of the bar in flack jackets and
insist that they were going hunting—folks like that.
Frank would never say a word. He'd raise one black
eyebrow at you to ask if you wanted another drink.
Never heard a sound from the man.

Joe would waltz Grace Heller around to "Please
Release Me" and get so fancy with his footwork that
the two of them would usually end up in the back
seat of my car before the night ended. The sisters
would sit on the phony hunter's laps eating cheese
popcorn and drinking cokes. The hunters could

never figure if the twins were of age, and might have suspected they were Macklin's daughters, so they mostly contented themselves with a few sly feels. I rolled the bar dice for shots, and once talked to the Indian girl about what it felt like to be an Indian. It didn't sound like much fun.

Macklin, once he was good and drunk, would make eyes at the muskie that was hung on the wall between the 'Gents' and 'Ladies'. He was in love with that muskie: a mounted, slickly varnished specimen nearly five feet long. The biggest ever hauled out of Stone Lake. Macklin would stroke the thing as though it were a sick puppy, burbling nonsense talk, while the fish, plastic eyes glaring out from its shiny head at the patrons in the bar, sat plastered in mid-swim where the taxidermist had frozen him. It was on one of those nights that the fish wound up wearing one of Grace's false eyelashes: a perfect row of black hairs curling above those vacant, angry eyes and that snarling jaw full of shellacked teeth.

So that's how the Spooner trips generally went. Each day Macklin would relax a bit more: he worried less about muskie and became content with catching respectable-sized bass; he gradually abstained from methedrine and booze; we knew he was in his best form when he took to wearing the sunglasses only an hour or two a day, and had genuine fits of heart-felt kindness like complementing me on my skills as a driver. A safe return to Chicago was then in order.

But last winter saw an end to the Spooner trips. It was an early fall, and an earlier winter. The flea markets closed up for the duration before I could unload the last of my swans: two yellow and a slightly chipped blue one. It was nearly three weeks before I landed my job at Tootsie Roll. I'm an extruder. An endless batch of chocolate goop comes down the conveyor into my station in the factory from the mixer. My machine, when it's running right, shapes this blob into sixteen ropes that head farther down the conveyor to Isaac Johnson, who runs the cutter. I can extrude fifteen, twenty thousand feet of Tootsie Roll on a good night, second shift. I'd been working nearly a month before Macklin, the sisters or Joe even crossed my mind.

One morning I got up early and headed up north to Macklin's flat. I knew he'd be home: all he did in the winter was take night classes at a college downtown, living off his disability pay from the Army. I could never figure exactly what it was that had been disabled; Macklin seemed healthy enough to me—in fact the wineheads that worked the truck docks at Tootsie Roll seemed in a lot worse shape. I wasn't about to ask Macklin about what the war had shot apart or ripped up, though. Everyone's entitled to at least one private disability.

So I went up to his flat one gray winter morning, took my boots off, warmed my hands over the radiator in the living room as he got me a good stiff drink before I realized he was in one of his "college moods." This affliction, when it had a solid grip on Macklin, usually after one of his night classes, caused him to forget how to speak normally. Trees became sycamores; cars were automobiles; my boots, for instance, were transformed into galoshes. "Take off your galoshes and have a seat," he had said to me. You can expect nearly anything from Macklin when he's in this mood: he's liable to talk economics, politics, or some other existential trash. I took the fat, gray easy chair that oozed stuffing from its arms and waited for him to return with the promised "libations." Macklin's wall of bass was behind me, looking out over me to the three bay windows with its closed blinds. I put my feet up on his coffee table next to a book entitled *The Angst of the Void*. I imagined passing Macklin's apartment at night, standing across the street at the Cuba-Mex driving school, looking up at the big bay windows, if he had them opened wide, and seeing all that bass staring back down to the street. Forty or fifty bass eyes peering down on Granville Avenue. Sort of a public service.

Macklin came in with stale potato chips and the drinks. Taking a chair at the window, he ran his bony fingers through what was left of his thinning blond hair. I noticed he was paler, had lost considerable weight since our last Spooner trip. He was wearing his sunglasses, despite the darkness in his apartment. His voice was thin, wiry. A few times when I brought up my job—how I was finally making good money—he tried to start in on how factory workers are oppressed by the upper class and used the workers as a buffer to keep the lower class in line, or some such shit. I changed the conversation to fishing.

"So where are the bass?" I asked, craning my head around to scan the collection. "You know, the two you caught on the last trip?"

Macklin got up, walked to the wall, stretched an arm toward the wall and said, "The two on the right. They appear as if they are preparing to bite each other. Mouths open."

I nodded. I kept the talk going with fish. I wasn't about to discuss *The Angst of the Void*, which

Macklin had recovered from the table and held in his
lap when he returned to his seat. He lit one of those
Italian cigars, tried to brush his wispy hair over the
bald spot.

"Last night," he said after a pause in our
discussion on what time of the year to use salmon
egg bait, "last night on the Granville el platform I
knew that I was Jesus."

I took a healthy gulp of my drink and saw that he
was not grinning. Macklin, I figured right then and
there, just might be worse off than one of his college
moods. He drew on his cigar, the lit end reflecting in
his sunglasses. I remained cool.

"I thought of my life, my deeds, of my friends, and
knew that I was Jesus—not THE Jesus," he insisted,
leaning towards me, jabbing his cigar at the air
between us, "just a minor one. I am Jesus because I
gather people. I take your sins. I lust after the
Litowski sisters but never, *never* have I, I," he
stammered , his pale face flushing with the rise of his
voice, "have never violated the sanctity of their
bodies. I keep them pure. I prevent the jackals in the
street from devouring them." He paused for a
moment and settled back into the chair. I emptied my
drink, sucked an ice cube up into my cheek. It had
snowed earlier, and you could hear the traffic slishing
to and fro on the street below. I had the feeling that
he had paused for me to say something, but what the
hell do you say to Jesus?

"I thought your mother has six kids. You were the
second or third. How can you be Jesus?" I asked. I
had heard somewhere that the best thing to do with
someone going over the edge, to keep them occupied,
is to reason with them. It was all I could come up
with on such short notice.

"You still don't understand. Not THE Jesus, but a little Jesus," he repeated, and attempted to show me just how little as he regarded a space between his upheld thumb and forefinger. "When I was up on the platform I could look the length of the tracks and down onto Granville Avenue below. A snow flurry was swirling through the amber street lights, the people passed below, hunkered against the wind, their collars raised about their ears, packages clutched to the hollows of their hungry stomachs," he continued, his head had lifted, sunglasses aimed at the bass behind me, his thin fingers wavered with the mention of snow flurries, tightened to a fist with the wind, and lightly pressed to his chest with the allusion to hunger. I restrained a belch.

"I felt exhilarated. I felt I was no longer of this earth, my body did not feel the cold although I could plainly see my own pantlegs flapping in the wind." He pointed his cigar at me once more as he said, "I saw, distinctly saw, individual snowflakes melt on my eyes, so many different angles, arches. No two alike, melting on my eyes! I took my hand from my pocket and saw that it was blue, the blue of a dead man's cheeks, and around this hand—I say *this* because I felt that it was a hand that no longer belonged exclusively to me—around it glowed an aura!" He showed me his hand, stretched it out toward me, palm up. No aura.

"Perhaps," he went on, his voice calming, "you've seen similar halos around car headlights in the fog. But when I gazed up from my hand, the people of the street carried these auras too! Each bent and tired soul carried this aura as a shield against the cold, and they did not seem to suffer the winds as much!" He paused as an ash dropped from his cigar onto his

pants, and he hurriedly scraped it onto the floor with
the edge of the matchbook he'd been holding in his
hand.

"And?" I asked. I knew Macklin was completely
gone, but I had become interested when he reached
the part about everyone on Granville Avenue owning
personal halos. Most people around there don't look
like they even own the spare change for a can of
soup.

Macklin removed his sunglasses and squinted at
me with his milky blue eyes. He seemed puzzled, as
though he'd forgotten something important.

"So what happened next, the people with the
halos and everything?" I prodded, leaning forward.

"Nothing," he said with a shrug and rubbed at his
eyes before replacing the sunglasses. "The 'B' train
arrived, and I came home. I listened to some Wagner
before turning in early."

"And just because you hallucinate that people are
running around with halos on their heads you think
you're Jesus? Lay off the booze, Macklin, lay off the
speed," I said. I'd become suddenly angry at him,
and I don't recall why. "Hallucinations on an el
platform don't even qualify you as a *little* Jesus."

"You could be right," he said. "This might not be
a religious experience at all. It could be
extraterrestrial. Extrasensory. Even sub-atomic. I
mustn't jump to conclusions."

I put on my coat and boots. It was time to get
help: Macklin was definitely going under. As an
orderly friend of mine once said, Macklin was in the
"black banana" stage: over ripe. I had to hurry out
to Joe's; a trip to Spooner was in order. It was
probably the only thing that would bring Macklin
around.

I stopped at a lone grocery-gas station on the highway outside the city. I knew Joe would need a few things out on the canal, he always did, especially when the weather was bad. The Cal-Sag canal runs to the city of Joliet, then down to the Illinois river; Joe's section is nothing but prairie, long stretches of vacant land dotted with factories. Joe owned over two hundred acres on the canal. Joe's father, Langston Matterling, had come up the Mississippi from New Orleans on a barge, got out at Joliet, and stayed on. He cleaned barges for a living, Joliet being the end of the line for many of them. When he got enough money he bought the land Joe squats on now, hammered together some piers for his regular customers to tie up at, and built quite a reputation for himself. He married, and the couple had one baby, Joe. One day Mrs. Matterling got fed up with living on the canal and with its snakes, green water, and Langston's fondness for cheap wine. She left. Langston died seventeen years later, while Joe was in 'Nam. Joe owned all the property now, free and clear. And he owned the family shack.

The shanty, perched near the piers, was built of old road signs, billboards, railroad ties and various doors, surrounded that day by tall, frozen prairie grass. Black smoke sputtered from a pipe on the roof. Joe's bike, his only means of transportation, was chained to the bumper of old man Materling's dead Chevy. Beyond the shack and the car, the land ended abruptly; three or four feet down was the canal, frozen solid. Bluish cracks in the ice ran from the abandoned, rotting piers out into the wide canal. A low, thin sheet of smoke settled into the grasses on the opposite bank. I went straight in without knocking.

I put the groceries, some beer, down at the table in the kitchen area. Joe looked up from the hot plate where he was fooling with the coffee pot. He'd grown a beard, looked thinner, and his flat-top had grown out. No sooner had the bag hit the table than he was poking around inside it.

"The heater," he said, motioning to the space heater between the washtub and where we sat, "the heater along with the old stove keep this place pretty warm, huh?"

The shack hadn't changed much. Joe's clothes hung on nails around the walls. There was the table with its hot plate, the potbelly stove, Joe's bed, electrical wire strung around the low ceiling of railroad ties, a spigot dripped a thin icicle into the washtub near the only window. The place was cave dark despite the blue winter light making its way in through the car windshield makeshift window and a lightbulb, shaded by a popcorn box, which hung over the table.

Joe popped a can of beer, and retrieving a can opener from the tangle of empty bottles and dishes around the floor, he opened a can of baked beans he'd dug out of my sack.

"What brings you out this way?" he asked, shoveling in a wad of baked beans with a slice of bread.

"Macklin," I said. How could he eat cold beans?

"Shit," Joe said with a laugh, and I noticed one of his front teeth was missing. I moved my feet closer to the space heater, knocking over a toy wind-up frog that had been sitting there next to an empty beer can. Joe leaned over, picked it up, cleared a space on the table for the frog, and set it down.

"Remember all these my dad used to collect?"

I sure did. The old man had maybe a hundred wind-ups at one time: a monkey in a pillbox hat that beat a drum, a polar bear that poured drinks from an XXX marked bottle, a squirrel that stole nickels from the limb of a tree, a worm that crawled a ruler. When we were home on leave one time his father dragged out the entire collection and wound them up. They flipped, zinged, stomped and chattered all over the shack, bumping and tussling into one another like a jar full of crazed guppies. One by one they'd wind down until the shack was quiet once again. Joe wound up the frog but it didn't move; it just sat there making chugga-chugga sounds. He opened another beer and began to use a spoon to get at the beans.

"So what's with Macklin?" he asked, running his tongue over his teeth, poking a loose bean through the gap.

"About to have a breakdown. We have to get him to Spooner. Quick. It might already be too late."

"You know Lake Michigan is froze over. Shore to shore, solid," he said, waving his spoon in the direction of the door and losing a bean onto the head of the frog. "That hasn't happened in over sixty years. And you want to drive to Spooner."

"Hey, you know it's the only thing that sets Macklin straight. I tell you, getting him out of the city, with the sisters and us, that'll bring him around."

"No way," Joe said. "We never went to Spooner for Macklin. You think a trip into the frozen north is going to cure him? Never did. Just made him more agreeable for a time."

"Then what do we do?"

"Nothing. We do nothing this time. Leave him be, maybe it's for the best." He clanked around the bottom of the can for the few remaining beans.

I even stay to the end of really bad movies. So I got the Litowski sisters' address from Joe and headed over to their place. I spotted them standing on the cold street, a block from their house sipping coffee out of plastic cups in front of a diner. I honked the horn and they climbed in. Marie, I think, had the black eye; it covered her whole eye socket and ran blue and brown down onto her wide cheekbone. Martha had blood caked around both nostrils, at the corner of her mouth, and on the lapel of her fake fur coat. They told me softly and slowly, as though they were reading a bedtime story to a child, of how their father had broken into their room the night before and had started beating on them. He was drunk, of course. They managed to escape and had been walking around ever since; they didn't have bus fare to Macklin's.

When I told them the state Macklin was in they didn't seem surprised. I said Macklin would take care of their old man once he was better. Martha shrugged, a fresh bead of blood on her lip; Marie gazed out the window humming to herself. We got to the north side an hour before I was due at Tootsie Roll. Martha let us into Macklin's flat with her key.

Since I'd left, Macklin had cleared everything out of the living room except a folding chair and the bass. He was sitting in the center of the room, completely naked, sunlight pouring in from the windows. Around him, circling the chair, were all the stuffed fish. Row after row of stuffed bass crowded around him as he sat pale and shivering in the center, ribs showing through his skin, his feet surrounded by cigar butts and ashes. He smiled at us, his watery blue eyes wide open despite the sunlight, wisps of his baby-thin hair rising above his head. First thing I did was call Tootsie Roll to let them know I'd be late. The girls, grabbing Macklin by the arms and side-stepping the fish, led him out of the chair. I phoned the local hospital and tried to explain what we had there. Meanwhile, the girls had coaxed Macklin as far as the hallway to his bedroom. He was limp and slow-moving in their arms, crouched over, tears running down his face as he smiled, a trail of matted hair down one leg indicated where piss had dried. I left. The Litowski sisters seemed to have everything under control, and an ambulance was on the way.

Now I know I was headed to Tootsie Roll; I had every intention of going straight to work. But I found myself in front of the Litowski sisters' red brick bungalow. I stopped the car, got out, walked into the house, and passing the T.V. set I grabbed a statuette of some religious person—I guess the Litowski's were pretty Catholic—and kept right on walking into the kitchen where I saw an unshaven, fat, oily-looking bastard leaning over a bowl of cereal. I think he wanted to say 'Who the fuck are you?', but I whacked him on the head, the neck and the face until he fell to the floor, spilling cereal over himself, his arms cradling his skull. I struck him a few more times, cracking a finger or two as they moved to cover his face. I let him alone then and walked out of the house, dropping Saint Jude or whoever on the snowy lawn, got in my car and drove away. Turned out I was only an hour late for work.

The last I heard, Macklin had been transfered to the VA hospital, and no one could say if he would ever be out. The Litowski sisters went to live with an aunt in Cleveland. But Joe lucked out. He sold his parcel of land in the spring to a dog food company and moved to Florida where he bought a condominium.

And me, I'm still extruding. I get another fifteen cent an hour raise after Memorial Day, and I'm on the company insurance plan now. I know it isn't as good as a condo in Florida, but it beats the hell out of counting the bugs on the wall at the VA hospital or living with a maiden aunt. It's a long way from selling ceramic swans, and besides, you can do a lot worse than getting off work smelling like chocolate.

I have vacation time coming up and it set me thinking of Spooner. I'd like to do it up right this time, so I sent away for brochures from the best lodges up there. I even sent letters to Joe and the sisters, but I doubt any of them will take me up on my offer. I bought a graphite rod and some great looking lures, still in the bubble packs, tucked away in my closet. And if I'm unlucky enough to hook one of those bastard muskellunges, I've got a brand new, stainless steel filet knife to cut the line.

Angela Jackson

The Blue Rose

The Hawk has eaten leaves from the trees that
stand between street and doorsteps. And young men
stand shivering on corners, their fingers pinching
close to the fire on cigarettes, which they pulled from
behind their ears. They have to have something
between their teeth—I think—to keep them from
grinding and gnashing their teeth to bitterest sand.
Something (cigarette, toothpick, reefer, wine bottle,
whiskey rim, lie) must be there to keep the nuisance
chatter of teeth muted in the awesome chill that is
more than something on the wind. It is early autumn
and should not be this cold. We college girls pull our
sweaters and jackets that come with the outfits
around our breasts. My nipples turn hard and I am
nervous.

We giggle and make small jokes as we saunter
through the dark, nodding congenially but quickly at
the doorway loungers and the judges of the stoop
who pass sentence on us. But the tactic of swift
politeness does not work. A lounger slides from his
position and matches steps with me. Why me?

"Hey, mama, what can I do for you?"

I can't think of one thing.

Trixia, who likes whoever likes you, says, "Hey,
brother." She is just the right casual. "Ain't this the
way to the best barbecue in the city?"

"Bone Yard the best. But Roscoe's will do." He is
very serious about food. "Yo hongry, baby?" he
breathes in my ear, determined to make me in his
family. His mama or his child.

"I'm looking for some barbecue," I don't turn my head cause I don't want to look in his nose. He's that close.

"I got a bone for you. The mambo sauce inside."

"That's too nasty," I sputter.

Leona joins in. "You ought to be shame."

Then Hamla recruits him, "Why don't you respect Black women and walk us to the place. Instead of talking that old talk?"

So he walks with us. He tells us his name is Berry, spelled B-E-R-R-Y as in the blacker the sweeter. He promises me he's sweet. His last name he says is Loomis. Hamla who used to be Camille Loomis observes him closely in the dark.

"I don't suppose we related."

"What's your daddy's name?" Berry asks with interest.

"George."

"And your mama's named Beatrice? And your daddy's got a older brother named Abraham," Berry is gleeful and talking really quickly now a genealogy of names nobody would or could make up out of the blue. "And the oldest brother Abraham had a son named Edward and Edward have a son name Berry and that's me."

"I think you my cousin," Hamla whistles.

"Gimme a kiss," Berry says angelically.

"I ain't that happy to know you," Hamla pushes him away. Her hand pressed against his chest. But he looks so sad, so she brushes his cheek with her lips.

Now we break past the shadow of trees lining the sidewalk, and moon finds us. Leona says, "Anybody know the man on the moon's mama's name? I bet you he colored and she from Mississippi or Alabama."

We are happy to be Black again, gliding through the nearly midnight streets. By now I'm sure we're not going to be back to Great Zimbabwe in time for the bus back to Eden, but that doesn't matter. We can glide back with grease around our mouths. The night's like that. Even Mrs. Sorenson the dorm mother who will put us freshwomen under house arrest when we come in late from the city doesn't phase us. Trixia will cry and lie for us about how we went just around the corner for something to eat and we didn't hear the last call and we got left and we was all alone in the terrible city. And it will be all right.

Roscoe's is next door to the Blue Nile, a basement blues club giving notice to the densely quiet street with a blue neon rose positioned on an iron bannister which leads to the cellar. When I see the notorious electrified rose blazing blue from roots coming out of the iron railing, I point it out to my friends from Eden and begin to tell the story of the Blue Nile.

I don't know who told me or told some one else I eavesdropped on, but the Blue Nile is the place for authentic blues. The owner, who was called Blue Nile before the club was, is a big, buxom, double-barreled woman, who's a cordial hostess who sets you up once the second time you come to her club. She's a smart businesswoman, honest as glass, and a connoisseur of the blues in its many shapes, especially the form which evolves along the Big River and shadows that river, then jumps a train, to the City by the Great Lake.

Sometimes people don't read the words and read instead the bright neon symbol that smokes when you get up close to it. Then they call it the Blue Rose instead of the Blue Nile. I don't know which name I like best: Blue Nile because it is ancient and I exult in the smallest survival, and like anything that's African, or Blue Rose because I've never seen blue roses and their existence here is improbable and evidence of miracles.

Sometimes, too, Miss Rose's boyfriend called her Blue Rose down at the garage when she sold fried chicken dinners (fried chicken, potato salad, spaghetti, green beans, salad, homemade pound cake, and two slices of white bread still smell fresh baked from the bakery around the corner; on the side, a personal mayonnaise glass of lemonade costing extra) which we delivered for her church's charity drive. "The poor giving to the poor," Mr. Boyfriend said as he tipped me and Littleson and Eddie before Eddie died. The mechanics, drenched in grease, would wipe their hands or not, pose the paper plates on their laps daintily like well-schooled princes and praise Miss Rose who they called Blue Rose or Miss Blue Rose, while blues rolled from the grease smudged jukebox in the corner that only played Jimmy Reed, Little Milton, BB King, Bobby Blue Bland, Dinah Washington, Joe Williams, a girl named Aretha Franklin, Billie Holliday and a woman named Mockingbird July singing a song I didn't know. Now that Mama and Madaddy had told me about her her name was everywhere.

The greasy mechanics lit into the church food, stuffing their mouths with crusty pieces of meat, slippery spaghetti, and buttery pound cake that left a film on their hands that blended into the film of oil already there. They licked butter and the blood of cars from their fingers, while we watched them like acolytes permitted the vision of gods at supper. It was

supernaturally romantic to hear Mr. Boyfriend call
my mother's friend Blue Rose; I knew then that
wonders were possible.

Maybe it was at Mr. Boyfriend's garage that I first
heard about the Blue Nile, also called the Blue Rose,
or maybe before then from the mouths of loud
talking and mumbling uncles, or women who tell
stories with the lift of an eyebrow and the purse of a
mouth, or maybe I heard about the Blue Nile
through my skin anywhere on Arbor Avenue or
around there, simply through osmosis.

No one's listening to my story of the club in the
basement where pipes sweat, washroom floors rot
and walls break in waves like the Mississippi River.
Not to mention the percentage of customers who are
low down and lecherous. Leona, Hamla, Berry,
Trixia, et al., are absorbed in the street noises and
characters who surround us and may mean serious
business. Each is poised for the sound or shifting
shadow that will come around the corner and say
RUN. It's rough around the corner from the Blue
Nile, which is where Roscoe's is.

The Blue Nile, the only bright spot on an
essentially residential street, is joined to another
building in which Roscoe's is located. Thick hickory
smoke billows out onto the avenue from a faulty
chimney. Leona says you could get drunk off the
smell of her daddy's mambo sauce and this smoke is
not the real McCoy. But Trixia says it'll do.

We are on the edge of the corner now, caught
between the smoke from Roscoe's and the sound that
opens up behind us as the door to the Blue Nile
opens up sending blue light and blues people and the
sound of Jimmy Reed ambling, "You got me

running, you got me hiding, you got me running, hiding, anyway you want me to go."

"Listen at that crying music," Berry, Hamla's lost and found cousin says of the sounds that come over our shoulders.

Everybody else just listens. I don't say anything. Do they remember what I do?

The Blues I remember from sounds spilled across the kitchen floor, pouring out the doors of the tenement on our street, seeping through the walls of Mrs. Wilson's Beauty Salon, next door to Mr. Boyfriend's place. Those blues singers I never saw (except on posters), like torn cats licking their wounds, healing on their tongues. But Berry, and I know, William, and the authoritative grad students would call that careful cleansing: the vanity of injury, the seductive canonization of the bruise, the dirty, defeated Negro slave music. Jazz is music (though few buy it) that is cool, cerebral, self-possessed and assassinating. Rhythm and blues our heartbeat. Blues is crime. Like a parent you're ashamed of and won't be seen in public with.

Jimmy Reed ends as we keep moving away from the Blue Nile. I want to know the rest of the song that slips up behind us in a different voice with lyrics like footsteps walking, "Jailhouse, crazyhouse, outhouse." The words keep tapping me on the shoulder. I want to turn around, turn back and go down those steps, touch the black railing and the outline of a blue rose and walk inside the light and smoke that roll out of the Blue Nile like fog around a river. But I keep going away, and turn into Roscoe's with the rest of the ravenous crowd.

I miss the waiters at Aisha Muslim restaurant moving like quick air, while the maitre de curved his back in brief elegance as he greeted the flock of us just flown down from Eden by way of the EARTH. As we clustered in the lobby, I strained over someone's shoulder to see into the dining room, a section of which was reserved for us, the tables covered in crisp white cloth brightened with red flowers and glasses of cold water served with a stream of courtesy. All of this waiting for us to follow the maitre de who bobbed as he bowed and fired out "Yes, sir," "Yes, Ma'am" in answer to our queries like we were all on film and he was playing in fast forward and the rest of us in slow motion. The maitre de ahead of our time; we watched the blur of his bow like a character in a Superman comic book.

On the other hand, the folks behind the tile counter at Roscoe's got no time to be pretty. So they act real ugly and look that way too. Mouths all tooted out in attitudes, rolling their eyes when the door opens and the bell tinkles our arrival. More customers. They're squinting and bumping into each other because spicy smoke backed up from the chimney is in their eyes. The little runty man with the prongs, and the woman with the spoon stirring sauce, and the boy shivering the basket of fries. I guess they think they're moving fast, but the motion here is desultory, like they're doing customers a big favor. We should know it's hot with the grease flying up from the bubbling baskets of fries and the glass pit that encases the ribs is hell to juke the long prong into to spear the right rib tip or slabs to slather with the sauce that'll do if you're desperate like we are and can't walk to the Bone Yard. We should know working at Roscoe's ain't easy, and just in case we don't know, they show us by being grouchy and bored. This is a bad night, I figure.

The chef-waitress leans on her side of the tiled counter and doesn't look at us through the window which she can't see out of anyway because of the smoke.

"Uh hmmm," she says to any one of us like she's finishing up an unpleasant conversation she began with us a while back and she knows anything we've got to say is aggravating.

Trixia orders a double order of rib tips with the hottest mambo sauce, fries with sauce and a strawberry pop. She and the woman dialogue real well. Trixia is turned side ways too, looking jubilantly at the piles of pork. The rest of us order the same way, turned kitty corner to the woman. Leona and I ask for chicken, thinking we'll appease the virtuous of the Aisha and Great Zimbabwe where pork is the embodiment of all racial evil, a slave sandwich.

Does it ever smell good. Knocking at our tastebuds.

It has begun to rain. No one anticipated rain. My mother and aunts would have pre-known the coming of the waters. The knowledge garnered in the loud ache of joints and bones. Our bodies are young and don't prophecy or remember much.

"When did it start to rain?" Leona asks with a little bit of awe making her voice go up like a little girl's. Nobody answers that, instead we talk about what the rain means. It is a harsh rain that looks like it's here to stay. Getting back to Eden, now that we've missed the bus, will be difficult. Perilous and slow, now that it's raining and past midnight too. We are not undaunted. So we give up the talk of our predicament and wait for the ribs.

The Blue Nile has separated me from my friends. I'm hungry like Leona and susceptible to the smell of pork; I'm wary like Berry who keeps looking at the door. I'm loud like everybody for a while. But the rain lends metaphor and atmosphere to my mood: melancholic and crumpy because I was not brave enough to walk into the Blue Nile unescorted. It goes on without me as a witness, the thing that makes "a man go crazy when a woman wear her shirt so tight. The same thang that make a hound dog howl all night" and I have missed it again. I am always amiss.

The day feels century-long. We came down from Eden in a covered wagon maybe, or more likely, we sailed down in a customized slave ship.

I have found a nook in the libraries of Eden, a Gothic terrible place looking like Dark Shadows, the daytime soap opera domain of Barnabas the vampire, Angelique the witch and sundry other monsters. We watched in high school when we got home from school early. I'm safe from TV monsters and Eden monsters in the cranny where Africana is stored. Eden is endowed with academic rights to West Africa and its Diaspora which means it has a department devoted to the study of Africans, and Africans from the Continent and white students from there and abroad make up the department. It's mostly white students. Most of the Africans (graduate students come to study engineering or political science) look sad or mad when I see them on campus. Steve, who's in the technological institute, runs sometimes with the Africans. The rest of us are too young for the Africans to bother with. Only one

or two are in For Bloods Only, but the grad students
of Blood Island from here are in the All African
Alliance (AAA) of Graduate Students of Eden
University.

The African section in Dark Shadows is the place I
love. Statues, with mouths, breasts and behinds that
toot out like mine, stand guard around the two
rooms, poised, some of them, with bent knees like
little girls about to jump between the curves of the
moving double dutch ropes. One statues has penis
and breasts like the picture of the hermaphrodite in
the anatomy book, but not so gross.

On one wall, just above my favorite seat, is a large
photograph of a Benin mask, a queen, with wide eyes
and mouth, wearing a crown of Portuguese soldiers
carved into her head. Like Excedrin Headache #99.
The original mask is in London. I have read this a
thousand times, inscribed beneath the photograph.
The original in London.

Underneath the hostage queen, I fell in love with
Joseph Cinque. Cinque was an African Prince
captured and on his way to America aboard a
slaveship. It was he who led the war of the Africans
aboard a ship called Amistad; who seized the vessel,
subdued the barbarian kidnappers carrying Bibles
and guns, and turned the Amistad back toward the
shores of Africa.

My newest acquisition from the Africana section
of the library of Eden is this love for Joseph
Cinque—another incendiary angel for a daydream.

Water races across concrete and slides over the
curb, stops at the blocked sewers and grows large
around the curb, swelling over and spilling back onto
the sidewalk. Who could navigate through this? I

look at us college girls. Are we the cargo or crew, bound for home or someplace ugly and new?

Then the ice babies come. They burst through the door and bring the cold rain in with them. They spin the water off their fake leather jackets, shake it out of their hair. One unwinds a red silkish scarf from round his do; it is soggy with rain. His hair sparkles. He wipes his dripping nose. He eyes us, shivers in the shoulders a bit, then leans toward us. We scrupulously avoid direct eye contact. The open door has let in a chill, so we wrap our arms round ourselves more tightly. We shift in our tracks.

Time is doing tricks again. The seconds accelerate and I know things are happening faster than I can make sense of them. But the dudes who just arrived follow the slow motion lead of the one with the red scarf. In decelerated time he drops the scarf at Berry's feet, like a kid playing "lost my handkerchief yesterday." We used to play that, a circle of us holding hands singing "Lost my handkerchief yesterday, found it again today. And then I threw it away." One of us, circling the circle, skipping behind us as we sang, would be holding a handkerchief which she dropped behind Whoever who in turn became It. And Whoever who'd become It would spin around and chase and chase the one who dropped the handkerchief. The dropper would be safe from It with the handkerchief only if she made it back to Its place in the circle before she was tagged with the handkerchief which was the reason for all this squealing.

For one micro-second I think Berry will pick up the scarf this dude has dropped in front of him and chase the dude all around Roscoe's. Jump over the counter and dance between the popping grease and

the smell of ribs. So he can tag the dude with the
scarf and be out of the game. But it doesn't go that
way.

Berry is It. All the wet boys jump on him and start
hitting him in the face and stuff. They shove him
back into a corner away from the counter and the
door and us and pommel him. The leader, spitting
through clinched teeth, "Told you don't bring yo
mug around here." He averages one strike per every
two words. I'm counting because this is slow motion
and my brain is careening along with the screaming
and pleading we're all doing for somebody to help
Berry, Hamla's long lost, soon to be dead cousin. The
woman behind the counter comes around and pushes
us girls back, because we're making crazy moves to
plunge in.

"Don't you get in this mess. That's all this is.
Nothing but mess."

Then she yells above the patter of fists and the
splatter of skin, "Get offa that boy. Doubleteaming
that boy. Stop it I say. Somebody call the police."

Berry is crunched up like a fetus being sucked out
the womb. He slings a fist out and twists out a kick
into the groin. One of the dudes pulls away, doubled
over, holding his self. His face jumbled up, yowling.

"Do you wanna burn?" comes a voice behind us,
quiet as rice steaming. And it's the wizened-looking
man who's been turning ribs. He's gripping the
handles of a huge kettle full of mambo sauce that
bubbles with heat, steaming so fierce he blinks
against the blindness.

"Whoever ain't' offa him in two seconds flat and
outta here in one, gonna be licking mambo sauce off
they behinds in the burn unit. So get yo ignorant
asses outta here with that shit. My name is Roscoe.

This ain't none of nobody's territory but mine, cause
I got the business here."

"Naw, brother," the dude who drops scarves for a
living says. "You must understand. This little
mawofuh knew his time was up. Maniac Apostles
run this. Taking what we come for." They turn to
grab Berry whose head is tangled between his legs.

"You ain't taking nothing but that nasty rag you
dropped on my floor," the man with the sauce says.
Then with no further warning, he flings the kettle of
red at them like a woman emptying wash water. We
girls cringe further into our corner, using our loudest
screams as talismans against the scalding liquid. The
Maniac Apostles streak past us shrieking like demons
shuttled back to hell. The sauce breathing equally
evil on the cold of their jackets. The rain slaps inside
and sprinkles us with grains of water that has turned
hard in the new cold.

*   *   *

"Maggie, it couldn't hurt to call."

"Go on and call him, girl."

We are in a world of trouble with no safe way
back to Eden. Leona calls Blood Island from the
Emergency Room; the yellow school bus would have
dropped everyone there before the tribes scattered
and fled to their dorms. We think Essie-the-cautious
might be sitting near the phone on the reception desk
waiting to hear from us. We are too wise to try to get
through to the desk at Wyndam-Allyn. Mrs.
Sorenson is on the look-out for lost Negresses, which
is what Trixia heard her refer to us as one day to one
of the residence counselors. Nobody answers the
phone at Blood Island, so us Negresses are consigned
to sit rescueless amid the smell of squandered blood,
bowel movements, and disinfectant in a hospital my

mother refused to give birth in and Eddie refused to die in. It's a quarter to three ante meridian. Berry the reclaimed cousin, saved and anointed by the murderously hot mambo sauce, sits bandaged and mildly sedated. He's checking in. Even though his burns aren't that serious and his bruises and taped up ribs will heal, he says he wants to cool out some, eat the nutritious, delicious hospital food and dream about the ribs from Roscoe's we never none of us got. Leona promises a ribtip special from the Bone Yard. She just has to ask her daddy and it is done.

Berry groans when Hamla hugs him for old times sake, touching his multiple bruises. "Sorry it had to be this way, little cousin," Berry apologizes. "I knew I was outta my hood over round Blue Nile and Roscoe's but I had to escort you pretty young ladies through Maniac territory. Specially when I found out you was blood. Couldn't let you go round there alone."

"Ain't nobody beat us up," I remind him more drily than I intend. He was only being nice. He tries to purse his lips in disgust at my ungrateful remark, but his lips are too swollen. Like humongous blueberries. I tell him we appreciated his company anyway. He didn't have to be the cavalry. "I might," Berry says, "be the calvary, or with this barbecue sauce on me be Grade A government inspected meat. I am A-1. If the streets don't get me the jungle will." He scares us good with his draft status.

Trixia who has to be the last word and have it too, flings her skinny arms around his braced thick neck and offers him a fervent goodbye that pops his eyes with pain at her embrace. She invites him to come visit us at Eden. "Just don't bring the Black KKK." Patience thins after midnight and no sleep, so Hamla snatches one of Trixia's arms and yanks her off the cousin in the wheelchair. Trixia is so into her scene she looks discombobulated. She curls up her hand real cute in a goodbye sign. The orderly wheels Berry away.

I wish somebody was riding me home safe to my own bed. Bring me in out the rain and the smell of blood and mambo sauce dabs that splashed up on my clothes.

Leona's daddy would kill her if he knew she almost got scalt to death at Roscoe's; not because she was in an imperiling situation, but because she was at Roscoe's, his chief rival's. So we can't call Daddy Pryor for a ride to the dorm. Nobody in Hamla's family has a car because they live right next to the el. Needless to say, nobody else knows a way, so they say "Maggie, why don't you call your daddy?" When I say no, they whine, "Maggie, why won't you call your daddy?"

I remember hearing my daddy coming around the rim of daybreak. The old stationwagon grunts along the avenue. This car is a chronic complainer, a noisy nag, beat up and dull, but I feel thrilled at the sight of it breaking through the darkness. My father thrills at the sight of it always and permits no one the right to sit at its wheel. In the days, last year, after I completed drivers' education he answered my thousand requests to take a spin with a hundred nos. And not one yes. Always his no. One morning he tore out of his room after I had been in there to get money Mama put aside to send away to Eden. He tore through the house up toward the front and peeked out the front window, after yanking up the shade. I guess his heart rested easy when he found his

car still there and me too. I'd followed up behind
him because I was just that mad that he'd think I'd
take his stinky old car. "You find what you lookin
for?" I said real sassy.

"You better nota taken my car, Maggie Lena," he
chuckled in his long johns, and barefooted back to
his room to say his morning prayers. Probably
praying for that car.

"Hi, Mr. Grace. Thank you so very much for
saving us from this terrible place. We got left by the
school bus, they wouldn't wait for us, then we ran
into trouble and Hamla's cousin got hurt and we
brought him here but we didn't have a way back to
school." My friends babble on as they hurriedly
climb into the car. My father acts as if he doesn't
hear any of their excuses. He yells, "Hey there!" real
jovially like when he walks into a room with a lot of
folks from Mississippi and he lifts his hand a little bit
in that country salute he and my uncles are good for.

I'm the last one in and I feel like It, a rotten egg,
or an old dead dog, the one that got left. I'm the only
one who knows the temper of this Grace in the
raggedy car.

"Thank you for coming to pick us up, Madaddy,"
I say without a hint of gratitude. My heart's beating
faster because I don't know how he's going to greet
me. In what way the embarrassment will come.
Through quick rebuke or rambling tale of childhood
peculiarities.

"Your daddy's so nice," Trixia says all satisfied to
be riding. "My daddy never would have gotten out
of his bed to pick me up somewhere. He'd a tole me
to stay my a.. behind where I was." The car is
crowded with giggles. The girls go into rough

imitations of their fathers who are not redemptive like mine. They are loud and entertaining and they win my father's approval. He smiles and chuckles behind the wheel. Then they start to tell him about our day. Before I can stop them. They begin at the beginning with the Cavebrothers who sleep with blonds of Eden, who will not be seen with beautiful Black girls like us, even if we wanted them to, then they take him to the EARTH and the terrible Alhamisi who we have decided by now is a known thug a little simple in the head and full of malice to boot. They do imitations of his warning us about the hippies who will turn in their hair and wind up as our bosses. Even though we agreed with Alhamisi about a log of things his style was so pompous and belligerent we give him no credibility. If he had worn a three piece suit and spoken softly with multisyllabic words we would have spoken of him with awe. As it is, he wore dirty jeans and looked unkept and uncouth and had a nasty attitude so Leona goes after him for handing out the commandments of Freedom Law.

"He thought he was Moses, Mr. Grace, coming down from the mountain with two tablets," Leona says, "I wish they'd a been some aspirin cause he gave me a real headache. He wanted us all to give up our educations and be farmers Down South."

My father says, "Back where I come from," then "Ah-hah-hah-hah-hah. Wooooh," he gives a little song that is his delighted and ironic laugh. Leona is a real hit with Madaddy. Miss Charm.

Then she and Trixia and Hamla fill him in on the fine cuisine at the Muslim restaurant and the music at Great Zimbabwe. I clear my throat but everyone ignores me. I try to talk about the grayness rising over the lake, to steer their talk away, but it's too late.

My father snarls, "You been over there eating that ignorant Muslim food. All them slick head zombies, goose-stepping like Prussian soldiers I saw over there in Germany. Where they oughtta be. Pack of crazy fools. Ain't good for nothing but eating stanky sardine sammiches and selling newspapers. Bunch of grown men ain't' nothing but paperboys. Littleson and Junior did that when they was twelve." He takes his eyes from the road long enough to do a full spotlight sweep of the car. "I hope none of you were taken in by any of that nonsense. That old nutty talk about a mad scientist inventing white people. If anybody but God invented white people it was the Devil, and the Negroes was right behind 'em in the line up."

My father fumes silently like a furnace. Then he pops, "Your mama's brother got caught up in that old mess." He is talking about my Uncle Blackstrap. What is unsaid now, but said loudly at home in the kitchen is "But a Dancer ain't never had good sense. Your mama included."

My friends make placating talk now about how the food at Aisha was so insubstantial they had to have some barbecued ribs to tide them over til breakfast which right now isn't that far away.

My father is appeased. "Maggie Lena always did like to suck on them barbecue bones." This is a lie, but I don't set it straight. It was some other daughter or son, but he wants it to be me so he can launch into a long humiliating story from my humiliating childhood. Which he does. He's telling the story of me and my best friend Jeannie who liked to fight and one time fought me over the right to suck my chicken

bone. Jeannie is married now. I don't guess she likes
to fight so much. I don't guess. Or maybe she does.
That's why she married a minor amateur prize
fighter. Feverishly I tune out the dumb tale from my
youth. I look instead at the way we came which is
even more startling as the way back. After all we
have seen.

Now Leona tells my father about the Man with
Two Wives and LeRoi "Get Down" Clay, who is a
poor man's James Brown. She is an amusing
anecdotist and soon has my father laughing. The car
is crowded with laughter. It bumps against me. Sam
Grace tells us he has been by Great Zimbabwe. He
peeked inside and smelled the incense that rushed
through an open window to meet him. He tells us
Great Zimbabwe is not nearly as fine as Club Desiree
was that night he took Mama, Aunt Leah-Bethel and
Uncle Blackstrap to hear Mockingbird July sing. It
wasn't the same magic place now, so he didn't go in.

When my daddy finishes the story I tell him we
passed the Blue Nile and I wished we had gone in.
His face is quietly happy and he makes no comment.
Then he clears his throat. "Hey, you ever hear this
song, Maggie Lena?" And he sings this song soft and
raggedy while I look at the light on the dark road
and listen. It is a song about a city by a river which I
do not remember well. Mimosa. It is a song about a
place where cotton grows, and figs, pecans,
persimmons (the per is silent) simmons, and blues.
About crackers and cottongins, trees, bossmen,
floods and fine women. All that will send you to
jailhouse, crazyhouse, outhouse. It's the hearthouse.

Jailhouse, crazyhouse, outhouse. I don't ask
Madaddy if he'd heard that song I eavesdropped a

snatch of as we passed the opening door of the Blue
Nile. He thinks all his little songs are original. So I
don't mention I've heard that line once tonight. It is
a pretty song, rough and sad like a painting by
Charles White. It is witty too like that man at the
63rd Street busstop who wears a rooster on his head.
The man sings and blows into his harmonica and the
rooster dances on his hat and my daddy's song is like
that. Sweet and magical.

We enter the outer limits of Eden and the cemetery
is on the left side of my daddy's voice. I imagine
those Black people buried there would rise up and
walk into the Great Lake like that lake is the
Mississippi River or the Niger. And some woman
ghost who came up at the turn of the century and
started to talk keener and forget her grandmother
who talked to animals, would do a sassy,
butt-swaying, foot-sliding dance on the jagged rocks
around the lake and look out over the water with her
hand curved across her eyebrows and smile.

I smile and fall into the safest sleep (a gentle sleep
so soft my eyelids feel like the inside of a rose), even
though we are only a few minutes from our beds in
the dorm room of Wyndam-Allyn. Those solitary,
non-communal beds. My own like a boat or a
private plane I love to float in. It is still novelty. Once
a week we strip those beds and leave the linen in a
pillowcase on the floor by the door. A woman,
brown as we are, only five years or so older than we
are, who lives in Eden a distance from the water will
pick up our bags of dirty laundry and leave freshly
ironed linen on our beds. She will scrub the toilets
and telephones at the ends of the hall, suck up the
debris from the carpet with her noisy vacuum, then
go home to a life like my own at home. Home. To a

mother like my own maybe, to a father who makes blues song a lullaby like my own maybe. To a chaos of kids and good things cooking; skin and bones covered in red sauce called mambo.

Life is good now for me and I stir in my sleep, catnapping on the edge of memory. Eyelids trembling, I wonder in the fog-soft edges of my contentment if this soft song would sweeten the rage of Alhamisi and The Earthmen, and melt the atmosphere of the Maniac Apostles who beat up on Berry who was family but who maybe was just like them with a different gang name. I sigh and burrow more deeply into the worn cushions of my father's car. This old car he prays for daily.

Tom Johnson

Litvak

Bro:

You should have been there. You weren't, so I'm gonna give it to you straight—at least as straight as the Seagram's that we shot afterward in the Legion bar. We hit those doubles down, one-after-another, and they splashed and burned, turning into acid and bile. Burned like those chemical drums out back of the plant that fizz and foam up until the poison leeches into the canal and river and boils up against the shoreline, washing in and out, bubbling like detergent, foamy and full of dead fish.

We buried Uncle Litvak today. He died from what Aunt Anna calls the "yellow death." She wasn't even surprised. He'd been a drinker all of his life and she always said that he'd drink himself to death. The liver finally got him. He'd been warned about it before. Remember when he changed from beer to scotch because that's what rich people drink? He figured it must be cleaner and better for you. Guess we ought to tell them Dewars people they ain't got the cure for cancer. He had cirrhosis all right. His liver was rock-hard and no good for anything at the end. You just couldn't believe the way he looked. His skin was yellowy as a bullhead's belly. Maybe it was that bullhead karma getting some kind of revenge. I'll bet he slit a few thousand of those suckers in his time.

You remember how he smoked those bulls in that little oven he built out back of the house? I remember the day when he brought home that big piece of tile pipe from the plant. Pa says, "What in the hell you gonna do with that, Lit? One single piece of pipe never did nobody much good. Ain't got a beginning and ain't got an end." But Uncle, he never answered Pa. I don't know what it was with them; something happened way back. Two guys who grew up on the same block and married sisters, you'd think they'd have a little bit to say to each other. But I don't remember them ever having a full-blown conversation.

Anyway, Uncle Lit, he just dragged that section of pipe out by the garbage burner in back and I tagged along after him. I can still see the grooves that the pipe dug in the gravel in the alley. I followed along, smoothing over the grooves, and he said, "That's good work guy, you fix up the alley where your uncle has screwed it up."

I asked him what he was going to do with the pipe.

"You just watch," he said as he set the pipe on end on the concrete slab where the garbage burner stood. Then, lickety-split, he banged a breathing hole in the bottom of the pipe, whipped up a bailing wire jig to set the fish on, and tossed a garbage can lid on the top.

"Hey Joe," he yelled up by our house to Pa, who was working in the garden. "Lookit me. Lookit the dummy Litvak. I'm makin' a planter outta this piece a pipe just like the hoy-polloy in Hinsdale. What a waste, eh Joe." Pa didn't answer and he couldn't hear Uncle's chuckle half way up the block, but he knew that he was chuckling. Just like Uncle knew that Pa was shaking his head, hitting each nail harder as he formed up the cold-frame he was building in the garden.

"You just watch, CJ," Uncle told me. "You hafta learn ta make do. Now, your father, he's one hell of a mechanic—a real first-class tradesman. But he figures that you have to do everything step-by-step, by-the-book, with all the proper tools and materials. Me, I learned somewhere, ya just gotta make do with whatever ya have handy at the time. We're different that way, me 'n him are."

Then he explained to me that you could set the meat or fish on the wire jig inside and the smoke would waft through and leak out at the top. "Yup. Now we have us a little ole smokehouse to smoke us some a that cat your Aunt has been cleanin' up for us."

He walked over to a pile of used lumber that he kept behind the garage and grabbed a few small scraps of wood that were too damp to burn. "Now you usually want dry wood ta burn, but when you're smokin', ya need damp wood ta get just the right taste."

He winked at me as he rolled the blocks of wood through the hole in the bottom of the pipe. I felt like he was letting me in on some culinary secret when he winked. When he balled up some paper to get the fire started, I could hardly wait. Then he said, "Don't get too impatient, guy. The smokin, it'll take a couple days, but it'll be worth the wait."

When the first wisps of smoke leaked through the cover, Uncle got down on his hands and knees and fanned at the choking fog with his hat. He coughed and spit a huge yellow wad into the gravel and then said, "That'll do her," as he arose. "An' soon we're gonna have us some smoked cat to barbecue with roasted patatas. How's that sound? Think your Pa 'll come over for some bar-bee-kew?" he said, drawing out the word so that it wrapped around me like the smoke.

Boy, could he barbecue. You have to remember that much. He'd take those smoked cats along with some potatoes sliced up really thin and wrapped in foil after he'd buttered and peppered them real heavy, and he'd throw the cats and packages of "taters" on his old grill that was caked so thick with grease and soot that you could have tarred a roof with it, and he'd work his magic. And he'd eat twice as much as the rest of us together, it seemed. Maybe it was all that smoke and grease and soot that gave him the cancer; or maybe it was just a case of "yellow death revenge" like Old Miss Varner said.

Talk about weird, you should have seen her in the back of the church, rocking back-and-forth and moaning in the back pew, wailing about nature getting even for all the world's evils and crap like that. It was hard to make out, because she whined sort of like a semi coming through the viaduct under the tracks, but everybody turned around to look and the priest dropped the incense burner right onto Uncle's face, lying there in the casket. Aunt Anna fainted and a couple people gasped and the whole damned ceremony felt real strange after that.

Look Bro, I know that I'm banging around here, but I'm just back from Uncle's funeral and I'm really drunk and tired and I just ate some speed so that I can say everything that I have to say. And I'm really pissed at you because you weren't there and because I've got to write this goddamned letter because you're out in the woods without a goddamned phone and pissed because in my heart I know Uncle Litvak was murdered.

Sure his liver was stone-cold dead. That's a fact which I don't deny one bit. But when they cut him for the autopsy, they found a cancer the size of a baseball. They were already certain that the cancer had metastasized throughout his whole body; that's why they didn't try to cut him to take the liver out. They said by cutting into it, it would have just spread the cancer more and he would have even been in greater pain.

The cancer had been in the liver for a long time. Maybe the bloated liver was defenseless against the invasion. I don't know. It doesn't seem as if anybody knows exactly how that works. They called the two-at-once an "interaction"—kind of like two cars hitting head-on rather than one hitting a tree. Either way, you get awful fucked-up. One is just more certain than the other'is all.

And then there was the fact of his retirement. Let me tell you about it. The bosses at the plant said they retired him early for his "convenience." That's what they told Aunt Anna when she called over there to tell them that he'd died. Thirty years of service, a little dinner over at the Elks, then it's "So long Litvak," on a lousy hundred and seventy-five bucks a month. Real convenient.

The day after the retirement dinner, he took me fishing down by that little place off Bluff Road where he liked to go. We looked at some bullheads and carp washing belly-up in the foam and he dropped his pole right there. It was like the first time he had really seen that kind of scene, though it's been bad for years and he'd been there hundreds of times before. But he seemed to look at it differently this time.

"Goddamn, I told 'em. I told 'em they were killin' us all, just the way they been killin' off the fish." He looked like he was watching his own corpse rotting in the wash along the riverbank. He just shook his head and uttered another "Goddamn em!" and we never fished again after that. That's what I'm talking about here.

He began to get really sick and slowed down a lot right after that. His skin loosened up and his muscles seemed to shrink and he took on the yellowish tint. His stomach started to swell; it seemed like it was bigger every day. And he lost the fight that he always had in him—all of the piss and vinegar.

Aunt Anna says that the retirement finally finished him off. We've all seen that happen around here with all of the layoffs and early retirements and shutdowns. People are made to be doing something is all; if they don't have anything to do, they just fuck up or die.

But the retirement was only one part of it. And I guess that he might have had half a chance against the cancer if he didn't have cirrhosis. Or vice-versa. He certainly had himself to blame for a lot of it. But goddamn it, Bro, they killed him. They're killing us all—the people who run the plant I mean. I know that I'm speeding my brains out right now, but I'm not being paranoid. They killed him the same as if they made him drink some of that tetrahydrochloride straight down. They killed him as surely as if they hung him from the water tower like we used to do with those stuffed dummies on Halloween. When the wind got through beating them around, they were just a bunch of flapping rags.

Uncle Litvak ended up disintegrating piece-by-piece until he was a bunch of hospital

clothes flapping in the breeze of an air-conditioner.
I'll never forget Aunt Anna saying, "He doesn't
deserve this. No one does."

Let me tell what "this" is: the room was a
standard hospital room at St. Mary's. Like all
Catholic hospitals, it had a crucifix hanging between
two television sets. Ma had pinned a St. Anthony
medal to Uncle's pillowcase. He was in the bed
nearest the window; he was still coherent enough
when admitted to demand a window bed so that he
could see into the woods across the highway. But
after awhile, he couldn't focus clearly much beyond
the bedside, so we'd have to tell him what the woods
looked like and what was happening in them.

He especially made a point to ask about the birds.
He could tell the season by the birds—the change of
seasons was the only time he seemed to care about.

Two plastic IV bottles hung above him on a
stainless-steel arm that looks like a plant holder. One
bag contained a saline solution to counteract
dehydration. The other contained a glucose/vitamin
mixture that was his last supper. Plastic tubes ran
down the wall, then along the bedframe, to his wrist.
The tubes were full of little ports where doctors and
nurses could inject medicine and drugs. The two
tubes intersected at a Y-shaped translucent plastic
fixture which hooked into a three-inch long needle
that was buried in his wrist under a gauze bandage.

Even when he was asleep, Uncle's left hand
constantly worked under the tangled clutter of the
plastic medical plumbing. He'd lightly and deftly
grasp the sheet with his fingertips as if he were a
seamstress. He must have used the same delicate
touch when he tied a fishing fly with a pheasant's
feather. Then he would open and close the hand like

he was squeezing a rubber ball. Sometimes he would grab the mattress or the bedframe and squeeze until his knuckles turned white and blue.

It was like that hand had a life of its own and was the only thing on him that still worked, that was still fully alive. Even when the rest of him distended into uselessness and withered away, the hand retained its likeness to a tree, gnarled and thick and bumpy as an aged maple or elm still rooted in the earth.

The hand never died; it was simply buried with the rest of the body as a matter of loyalty. Uncle Litvak's hand is immortal. What happened to the rest of him is criminal.

The last of his life just dripped away. A catheter ran from his penis down the side of the bed into a plastic bag that filled with a mixture of blood and piss. Each day, the bag filled more quickly and the mixture became darker. It started to look like malt liquor after awhile. Another bag hung next to the pee-bag. It was the receptacle for the tube that ran into his lungs and flushed them out. The fluid in that bag was clear and bubbly.

From time to time, a nurse would have to run a tube down his throat and vacuum it out when it became clogged with phlegm and fluid. Saline, glucose and drugs in. Piss and blood, lungjuice—out. He went out as bad as you could, I guess; except that he was really heavily drugged and maybe didn't feel some of it.

Once, we were there on a visit and he was asleep. Ma and Donna and Benny and Shelly went to get something to eat, so Aunt Anna and I were there all alone. That's when she told me about Uncle's fear of hospitals. She said that she found out about it when he got home from the war. When Aunt Anna told me this, it was like he was telling her again for the first time. I could see real blind terror in her eyes.

She'd been staring at him and the phlegm gurgled in his throat—it's called a "death rattle" according to Ma. It's a dying person's way of telling you it's almost time.

Anyway, Aunt Anna stared him right in the face and she said, "I want to look right at him when he goes." Really made me feel funny, like she was scolding him or something. That's when she started to tell me about the nightmare.

It was like she stepped right into his head and was seeing the dream herself. She was looking right at her husband and watching him in the throes of dying and she started telling this dream that she heard only once in her life, forty years ago.

She said it had been waking him up nearly every night after he got home from the war until finally one night she told him: "Lit, you tell me about it, what it is, or I'm going to leave. I can't live like this. I know it has to be bad, but you've got to tell me. I know I probably can't understand, but I have to know what it is. You have to try, or I'll leave, I really will."

Aunt Anna told me this like it was happening all over again. And then she just started telling the dream and I'll be damned if wasn't Uncle's voice I heard coming through her mouth:

"I'd go into this brick building painted olive-drab that looks just like a VA hospital. I'm walking though the door and even though I know I'm inside, I can see the place from the outside. I hear this thump land beside me and I think a newspaper boy on a bicycle has just thrown a newspaper to me. But I look down to pick it up and it's a man's arm. It has

a tatoo on it: a bright yellow rose underlined with
scroll lettering that spells out TEX. It belongs to Tex
Joplin from Galveston. He died next to me on
Omaha Beach. Then a leg comes flying out a
window. Another arm flies out.

"A whole body, piece by fuckin' piece. More
bodies. Then some orderly empties out pieces of
body parts and buckets of blood from one of the
windows.

"And there are these doctors. They're dressed in
white coats and wear these big round silver discs
stuck into their foreheads with thermometers. The
doctors all lean out the windows and laugh and start
yellin' 'WE GOT OURS! WE GOT OURS!' like
cheerleaders or somethin'. And the bodies keep
gettin' tossed out the windows and pile up like at a
junk heap.

"I walk up to the pile and it looks like my own
body is right on top. I can tell from the uniform
blouse that it's me. All of my medals are pinned
above the shirt pocket—a purple heart, campaign
ribbons, a silver star and some others. And there's
this medal of the Sacred Heart of Jesus pinned with
the rest, only it's alive and bleeding. Now I'm sure
that it's me. That's scary enough. But then a head
rolls from the body and stops right at my feet. It
belongs to some kraut officer that I killed later on.
Just a kid—they had kids fightin' then. Ya know, I
still got that kid's dagger hangin' in the basement
with the other souvenirs. It's a fancy thing, the
handle swirls just like butterscotch in a fancy
candy-store. There's a swastika engraved on the hilt.
I guess that's why I kept it. It'll probably be worth a
lot some day. Anyway, this kraut's head that's layin'
in front of me, it's got its ears sliced off and blood is

pourin' from the holes and it stares at me. Each and every goddamned night. That's why I wake up in a sweat."

As she related the nightmare, I wondered if maybe he was listening or something. You know, how you sort of half-hear things when you fall asleep on the couch watching TV or reading the paper. But Aunt Anna looked up at me like she was reading my mind and said, "Don't worry; he's unconscious almost all of the time now. He hardly understands anything. Yesterday, he didn't even recognize Benny and Shelly, his own children."

It still made me feel pretty funny though, talking about him like he wasn't even there, like he was in the coffin already dead. I felt like I was a priest in a confessional.

But I guess she had to tell someone; she had to get it off her chest. I just happened to be the one there, so I sat and kept my mouth shut and waited until Aunt Anna's voice faded away.

I looked out the window into the woods where we used to play. If you look really hard, you can see the toboggan slide over on the Heights. The kids still use it all year round like we did. They still go up there and get drunk behind the pumping station and find a piece of cardboard or whatever and slide down the chute, laughing and screaming, and probably burning their skin through their jeans like we did. Remember how you always had to cool off Ma when she yelled at us about tearing up our clothes?

You had a way of quieting her down so she wouldn't tell Pa and we wouldn't get our asses kicked. You always could get us out of it. So where are you now? You should have been here when we needed you. When I needed you, you motherfucker.

When I had to sit there with your dying godfather
and remember what it was like when we were kids,
staring out that hospital window because I couldn't
look at him. I needed you.

But I guess hiding out in the Colorado wilds does
have its advantages. Nobody ever told him that you
quit med school and went off into the woods with
Lana to live the pure life or whatever the hell it is
that you do out there. But you're free, huh. Free
from your family and its clumsy ways. Free to
envelope yourself in nature and all that shit. Free to
sit on your ass and meditate. Well, meditate on this
Bro—your godfather is dead and this whole
goddamned town is following him right down the
tubes.

And me, I'm trying to ride out this black beauty
that I ate. Goddamn. I promised him when I threw a
dried up Easter Lily onto his coffin that I'd give it to
you as straight as I could. He would have wanted
"the doctor" to know everything. He told Aunt
Anna once: "Don't worry babe, I ain't gonna kick
off. I'm just waitin' for the 'doctor' to come home
and fix me up once and for all."

Now it's too late to fix him up. He knew he was
dead the day after his retirement when he and I went
to the riverbank. That was when it all stopped for
Litvak Janus, president emeritus of Legion Post
559—the Ralph Sikorski Post. Litvak Janus of
TransCorp USINC, retired. Litvak Janus who said it
straight: "Goddamn 'em. I told 'em. I told 'em they
were killin' us all the way they were killin' the fish."
The day when his spit fizzled in the foamy water
while the dead fish floated belly-up was the day your
godfather wrote his own epitaph. Hell Bro, he wrote
all our epitaphs.

Goddamn it, somebody has got to even up the score. Even it up soon. Even it up even. I'm tired. Tired of this letter and wakes and funerals and slow deaths. Tired of murder, whether it's with guns in the street or a corporate poison-the-world program. Tired enough to do something really crazy because craziness makes a lot more sense to me than this insane silence which surrounds us. Tired of standing by, while we watch ourselves being murdered. If you're with me Bro, get your ass back here—pronto.

Your Momma's Other Boy,

CJ

Maxine Chernoff

The Untouchables

Jane knew that her father, a leather goods salesman, was of the merchant class. She had been studying the caste system in school and worried that working with leather put him in jeopardy since Untouchables dealt with animal skins. As long as her father sold leather he'd be safe. Salespeople were never Untouchables. She would have liked her father to have been a Brahman, but after all, her family lived next to a gas station and showed no particular interest in learning or religion. Usually this pleased her. While her Catholic friends were tortured in Sunday clothes, Jane could ride around the block on her old Schwinn bike singing "Some Enchanted Evening," her favorite song from *South Pacific*. Every time she passed the Shell station, she'd ride over the hose that made the bell ring. Sometimes it punctuated the song mid-chorus. Other times it accompanied her as she reached for a high note. When she got bored, she'd park her bike, walk back to the gas station, put her quarter in for a Coke and swig the bottle down leaning against the red metal housing of the machine. No one noticed her. She could stare at anyone she pleased. Mostly she looked at the *m'woman*, which was what her father called the person who pumped gas on weekends.

Jane had concluded that the man/woman was definitely a woman because the badge on her shirt didn't lie flat over her breast pocket. It puckered as her own pockets had begun to lately. But no woman in her right mind would have shaved her hair way

above the ear or that short on the neck and let grease
accumulate all over her face and hands without
trying to clean herself up. Once Jane asked her
mother about the *m'woman* but was told to be quiet.
If she'd followed with "Why?" one of her parents
would have said "Why is a Chinaman's name,"
which had never made any sense to her. Victoria
Pranz's mother had told Jane that the *m'woman* was
probably a lesbian. Victoria's mother was definitely a
Brahman, an art professor at the University of
Chicago, though her status was questionable
considering her recent divorce.

Dr. Pranz would be a Brahman too, Jane
calculated, by virtue of his classical music training.
Even though he'd given up the flute to practice
dentistry, he might have played in a symphony. Once
Victoria had told Jane that dentists have the highest
suicide rates. From then on Jane had stared at Dr.
Pranz, trying to detect a sudden sadness behind his
jocular manner and jaunty little Van Dyke beard.
When he left Mrs. Pranz, Jane wondered if he'd take
to aimless wandering along Lake Michigan until a
surge of emotions vaulted him into the water. But
when he came to pick up Victoria on Saturdays, he
never looked anything but animated. Sometimes he'd
include Jane in a special outing. En route he'd hum
to the classical music on the car radio. One morning
they'd gone to Calumet harbor to tour a merchant
marine ship from Denmark. Someone depressed
couldn't have thought of such pastimes. Jane's own
father, absorbed in the Cubs' problems with
lefthanded hitting or bills or edging the lawn, looked
far sadder than Dr. Pranz. Perhaps Brahmans were
naturally more content than the merchant class.

On Sundays Victoria and Jane rode their bikes together. On the particular Sunday it happened, Jane was in the lead, Victoria well behind. That was a difference between them. Victoria dallied, taking in details, reserving judgment. Maybe she'd inherited her mother's preoccupation with seeing. Jane remembered a horrible Columbus Day spent at the Art Institute with Victoria and her mother, who paused for one, sometimes two minutes, at every painting before moving on. Even worse, Mrs. Pranz asked Jane what she thought of several Cezannes, as if Jane could tell her something she didn't already know. "You're the artist," Jane had finally said when Mrs. Pranz seemed dissatisfied with her replying, "I think they're okay."

When Jane went over the gas hose this time, her tire skidded in some grease and she went flying over the handlebars, landing on both palms and knees. Before Victoria caught up with her, the *m'woman* had rushed out of the gas station and was helping Jane up. She made a greasy fist around Jane's forearm. Pulling Jane to her feet, she surveyed the damage. "Guess you'll be all right," she said and offered Jane a new flannel cloth. Jane stared at her palms, which were red and smarting under the grease, and at her poor knees, which had taken the brunt of the fall. One was bloodier than the other. Jane dabbed at them with the rag. Before Victoria arrived on the scene, the *m'woman* had walked back into the garage.

"She talked to me!" Jane told Victoria as they walked their bikes home.

"Who?" Victoria asked, cocking her head like her mother while waiting for the reply.

"The *m'woman* came out when I fell. She has a lady's voice. She gave me this cloth." Jane held it toward Victoria's hand.

"Yuck," Victoria said.

By then they'd reached Jane's house. As Jane expected, her mother asked Victoria to go home. Whenever Jane got hurt, her mother used the occasion to lecture not only about safety but whatever had been on her mind since the last injury.

"Let's go to Woolworth's," her mother said, wiping the last grease off of Jane's legs. "I need some yarn, and I'll buy you a vanilla coke."

Bandages on both palms and knees, Jane limped to the Fairlane. She made a half-hearted effort to comb her hair and wet her lips shiny as her mother started the car and headed of.

"Jane, I was wondering, honey, whether I've told you enough."

"About what?" Jane asked, recognizing a very different line of questioning.

"About growing up," her mother said.

"I guess it's just happening anyway," Jane said looking down at her hands, which, with the extra bandages and the stiffness they caused, appeared huge.

"I mean something else," her mother mumbled. Why wasn't Mrs. Pranz her mother? She had brought home a gynecological text and taken Victoria to a health seminar on her eleventh birthday. Whenever Jane's mother wanted to talk about sex, she got all self-conscious and stuttery and even drove funny.

"Mom, you're going twelve miles an hour. I think the speed's at least twenty-five."

"Do you know about babies?" Jane's mother blurted out as she parallel-parked the car in front of Woolworth's. Parking had taken three tries.

"They're those little things with diapers, right, Mom?"

Before her mother could answer, their attention was caught by the contorted couple standing in front of Woolworth's. The thin young man had his arms around the girl, who was younger still, perhaps sixteen. Her hands were tucked demurely in her pockets. What fascinated Jane was how their bodies connected at the tongue, and how they twisted against each other for what seemed like forever.

"They're Frenching," Jane explained to her mother, who looked either confused or stricken. "Hey, that's Nina Treesom!" she added. Nina lived across the alley and had been dating a college boy.

"Hi, Nina," Jane said, as her mother whisked her past them into the store.

"Yarn?" her mother asked, a tired monosyllable. The woman pointed them toward the back of the store, Jane's favorite area, where she could watch the parakeets crowding together, chirping on their perches.

Her mother bought pink and blue and yellow mohair, promising Jane she'd make her a sweater. Every so often she took on such projects, but most ended in failure. There was a whole box of half-made sweaters and scarves in the bottom of the linen closet. Jane said that would be nice, but spent her time over the vanilla coke thinking about the *m'woman*. After the flannel cloth was clean, Jane would return it to her. Maybe the *m'woman* would explain to her why she dressed that way. Maybe she

was from another country, but Jane hadn't detected
an accent.

"The couple you saw outside Woolworth's," her
mother began after getting behind the wheel, "had
better be careful." She was shaking a manicured
index finger toward Jane's nose.

"Mom, that was Nina. Remember, she used to
walk me to school when I was in kindergarten?"

"Nina or not, one thing leads to another."
Squinting to look serious, she added, "Remember
Tammy Schwartz?"

"Yes," Jane said, recalling Mrs. Schwartz's hefty
daughter who'd gone away one summer to work at a
resort in the Wisconsin Dells.

"She didn't go to college after that summer, Jane,
like Mrs. Schwartz told everyone. She had a baby."

"But she wasn't married."

"I'm telling you, Jane, it's dangerous to be a
woman." She was looking crazed again. They took a
sharp left. The tires squealed around their corner,
engraving the afternoon on Jane's eardrums, and they
were home.

Jane lay on her bed and wondered whether the
m'woman worried about such matters. It would be
nice to worry about nothing at all or just dumb
things like her father did. Jane wondered what the
m'woman's status would be in India. Then she
remembered that unmarried women were always
disgraces to their families.

When Jane walked into the gas station garage, the
m'woman was reading the Sunday paper and
smoking a cigarette. She had stretched out her legs so

that they rested against the edge of the counter. Her workboots provided traction.

"Excuse me," Jane said.

The *m'woman* looked up and smiled at her.

"I have your cloth." Jane held it towards her.

"Thanks," the *m'woman* said. "Are you all healed?"

"I'm fine," Jane said. Jane noticed that the insignia over her pocket read "Ike." She smiled to think that Ike and the president shared the same name.

"I'm Jane."

"I'm Sheila."

"Your pocket says 'Ike.'"

"I'm Sheila Ikenberry. People call me Ike."

"I'm twelve."

"I'm thirty-two."

Then the gas bell rang, and a blue Chevy was waiting at a pump.

"Right back," Ike said.

Jane picked up the paper Ike had been reading. It was folded at the classified car ads.

"I'm looking for a car," Ike said.

"My dad buys Fords."

"Right now I have a Studebaker." She pointed outside to a two-toned sedan colored like toast with jelly. "It's getting kind of old, and I live way out in the sticks. I need a more dependable car for winter."

"My mom drives my dad's car. Someday I'll probably have my own car. I wouldn't mind a Thunderbird."

"Right now your bike is fine, I'd guess."

"Sure, it is. I'm talking about the future."

"What do you want to be in the future?" Ike asked.

This is leading somewhere, Jane thought. If she just said the right thing, Ike would explain herself. "Maybe a truck driver," Jane said, hoping to prod Ike along.

"When I was little, I wanted to be a nurse."

A Plymouth pulled up. The man got out of the car and walked into the gas station.

"Got some change for the Coke machine?" he asked. Ike gave him four quarters for his dollar.

"Your hair's pretty short," Jane said while the man was opening his Coke.

"Yeah, it's convenient for me that way." Ike picked up her paper and started looking down the column again. "I used to wear it longer when I was your age." She drew red circles around two car ads in a row.

"Do you have any pictures?" Jane asked.

"Of what?"

"Your family or how you looked before you cut your hair."

"Not on me," Ike said. "Why don't you come by next Sunday? I'll bring a photo of me when I was your age."

"I'll try," said Jane. "Mostly I'm free on Sundays."

"Want a Coke?"

"I don't have any money."

"I'll treat you to one," Ike said, "and then I have to close up for the day."

All the time Jane drank the Coke, she watched Ike reading the ads. Ike never looked up or seemed to notice that Jane was staring. If she did notice, she ignored it, just as she did Jane riding over the gas station hose again and again.

That Tuesday Mrs. Pranz took Jane and Victoria back to the Art Institute. In one gallery right near *American Gothic*, which Jane remembered from her previous visit, she saw a painting she hadn't noticed before. It was a gas station painted at night by someone named Edward Hopper. The station itself was lit up and the majestic red pumps topped off with white globes. There was a lone attendant standing at one edge of the painting and a road that went off into darkness. Jane liked how the painting admitted that gas stations mattered. She hoped Mrs. Pranz would ask her about it. For once she'd have had something to say.

On the way out Mrs. Pranz asked the girls what they'd like in the gift shop. Victoria picked out some stationery with Degas dancers. Jane chose a few postcards. Between a Renoir mother and child and Van Gogh's homey bedroom, Jane slipped the Hopper painting.

Because it was raining that Sunday, it was harder for Jane to get out of the house. She knew she couldn't just say she was going to the gas station or mention Ike's name, even as Sheila Ikenberry. She was glad for one thing. Her mother had gotten all involved in the sweater and forgotten about Jane's education in being a woman.

"I'm taking a walk," Jane said. Her father, who was reading *National Geographic*, didn't look up.

"In the rain?" her mother asked, peering over her glasses.

"I need a few things at Woolworth's," Jane said, "and I want to look at the parakeets."

"Don't look too long," her father said, "or they'll charge you."

She ran the distance from her house to the gas station. Ike was exactly where she'd been last week. She was wearing a rubber raincoat over her slacks and shirt.

"Lousy weather to pump gas," she said when Jane walked in. "On days like this I wish I *had* been a nurse."

"I guess you still could be," Jane said but regretted it immediately. It was the kind of thing her mother would have said to cheer someone up.

Ike smiled and opened the drawer under the cash register. "Voila!" She produced a picture of herself as a little girl. "That's me at six. I couldn't find me at twelve. Pretty cute, huh?"

She was sitting on a stuffed bear at a zoo. Her hair was short and the little skirt she wore revealed thick, sturdy legs. Because she was smiling into the sun, her face was wrinkled up.

"Where was it taken?" Jane asked.

"The Bronx Zoo. That's where I grew up. Not in the zoo. In the Bronx." She laughed.

"Why did you come to Chicago?"

"Just to follow a friend. The friend was going to move here, so I did too."

"Where's your friend now?"

"That's a long story." Ike looked out the window.

"I brought you something," Jane said, reaching under her rain slicker and pulling out the postcard. She placed it on the counter next to the cash register.

"A postcard of a gas station," Ike said. "Now when I'm at home, I'll be able to remember where I work on weekends." She laughed. "It's really very nice, especially those old-fashioned pumps."

"It's of a painting at the Art Institute."

"Right. A pretty nice painting."

"I go there all the time with Victoria and her mom. Her mom's an art professor."

"I saw you yesterday with your mom. Pardon me for saying this, but your mom's driving leaves something to be desired."

"She just learned two years ago. Believe me, she's gotten better. Did your mom drive?"

"My mom didn't drive and neither did my dad. My older brother drove though. He taught me one summer."

"Why didn't they drive?" Jane asked.

"You ask a lot of questions," Ike said. "How about a little break? Can I buy you another Coke?"

They were at the machine when Jane saw her father approaching. He was wearing a rubber raincoat identical to Ike's.

"Jane, you're wanted at home," he said.

"Dad, this is Sheila Ikenberry."

"Pleased to meet you," he said, turning to hold the door for Jane.

"Do you spend a lot of time there?" he asked when they were out of the rain under the overhanging porch of their house.

"Not really," Jane said. "Ike saw when I fell off my bike. She came out and asked if I was all right. I guess that got us talking."

"You know, Jane, there's something strange about that woman."

"Daddy, you call her 'the m'woman.' Anyone can see there's something strange about her."

"You probably shouldn't hang around there. Let's not tell Mom for now. She's off in all directions with worries."

"Yeah, what's her problem?"

"Well, we didn't tell you, but for awhile we thought that she might be having another baby. Then we found out that she wasn't."

"Is that why she needed yarn?" Jane asked.

"No, she needed yarn later. After she found out she wasn't going to have another baby."

"Why would you want another baby," Jane asked, "when you have me?" For a reason she didn't understand, she felt tears forming in her eyes. She knew her eyes turned greener when she cried. She didn't know if she was crying because she wanted her parents all to herself or didn't want them at all.

They were standing in the foyer when her mother asked where Jane had been. Her father held his finger to his lips, looked Jane in the eye, and said, "Oh, just around the neighborhood. I treated her to a Coke at the Shell."

The next Sunday Jane looked up Martinegro's Shell Station in the phone book. When Sheila Ikenberry answered, Jane said she thought she'd just say hello. Then she told Ike that her mother was going to have a baby but that things hadn't worked out.

"I mailed that postcard to my friend," Ike said. "You know, the one of the gas station? I thought she'd get a kick out of seeing what I've made of myself."

Susan Lynne House

A Tin of Tobacco Under Her Wing

Hazel Boggs had come a long way. Chicago was far from Nova Scotia and the Creative Space Center was far from the fisherman's cottage she'd shared with her first husband. She remembered rhythms: the beat of the waves against the huge rock under their cabin, the daily pull of the tides and the annual shifting of the seasons, the pulse of tourists as they spread across the rocks from their buses and then funneled back into them, and the churning of the motor on Guy's trawler. She also remembered the day the motor quit and Fundy's tide pushed Guy's boat onto the rocks of Brier Island.

Hazel had left the cove then. Where once she'd seen stark and unexpected beauty in the massive boulders torn from bedrock and scattered by glaciers, now she saw only a moonscape. Where once she'd felt the grinding power of the glaciers in their lovemaking, without Guy she felt only the deadly spread of the ice. Hazel ran from the sight of the dock where the mooring ropes for Guy's boat hung uselessly. She ran from the empty horizon and from the pillow she clutched at night when her arms ached to hold Guy.

She moved to New York City and got a job as a French translator in an insurance office; but the salty smell of the ocean would occasionally penetrate New York's pollution and reawaken her memories. The press of the crowds on the street, the pressure of office politics, and the speed of life in the city all bore down on her when she smelled the ocean. Hazel ran again. This time into marriage with Jim Boggs, an insurance agent from Missouri she met when his sales had won him a trip to New York. The marriage gave Hazel new rhythms, new scenery, and no smell of the ocean, but Jim drank too much and their lovemaking did not move her. She began to feel as old and worn as the Ozark Mountains where they lived. One day as she was weeding her flower beds, she heard the grind of a truck's gears as it strained its way up the mountain. She rose from her knees and walked toward the road. As the truck neared, Hazel stuck out her thumb. The big truck slowed and stopped and Hazel swung herself into the cab.

It was quiet inside. Hazel looked at her hands, at the dirt from her garden under her nails, at the stains on the knees of her jeans and, finally, at the driver.

"What's the matter, honey? You lost?" The driver asked.

Hazel stared, speechless, at the tall woman who sat behind the big steering wheel.

"Well, guess you won't be real exciting company," the woman said as she eased the big rig into gear and back onto the road. "Wanna tell me where you're headed?"

"You're a woman!" Hazel blurted.

"You ain't too fast, but I guess you're not blind." The tall woman smiled at Hazel. "I'm hauling this load to Chicago. Were you going that way?"

"Yes," Hazel said, "At least, it's okay if I go there. I'm Hazel Boggs."

"Okay, Hazel Boggs, we're going to Chicago. I'm Lu Richmond."

Lu drove and talked all day. She seemed content just to have company in the truck. Hazel relaxed as the sound of Lu's voice and the hum of the tires began to form a new rhythm in her mind. They stopped for the night in a motor inn just outside of St. Louis. Somewhere south of Springfield, Illinois the next day, Hazel began to talk, and she talked all the way to Joliet. There was something about Lu that made Hazel feel safe, made her able to open up and talk. She told Lu about the red soil on Prince Edward Island where she'd grown up and about the university in Nova Scotia where she'd met Guy. She told of her first sight of the rocks in Guy's hometown, boulders, bigger than houses, tossed randomly by a giant's hand. Hazel talked for the first time in ten years about Guy's death and she felt it ease its grip on her heart. Lu's listening eased a decade of pain in Hazel.

They stopped at a truck stop near Joliet and when they resumed the trip, Hazel continued her story. She talked all the way through her years in New York and her marriage to Jim. At last, she talked herself into the cab of Lu's truck. When Hazel finally fell silent, she was exhausted and slept the last hour into Chicago.

They were in an industrial area of the city when Hazel awoke. She looked out first one side and then the other of the truck and saw nothing but gloomy gray buildings in every direction. Hazel could feel panic begin to rise within her.

"You got any people here?" Lu had noticed Hazel's discomfort. "I'll take you to them as soon as I check this truck in."

"No." Hazel's voice sounded small.

"Where you gonna stay?"

"I don't know." Hazel looked out the windows again.

"Seeing as how I brought you this far, I guess you could bunk at my place for awhile." Lu said as she steered the truck into a large lot. "Look, I've gotta check this thing in, you hop on out and walk down to that diner on the next corner. See that pink sign down there? I always pop in there after a trip. You tell the waitress Lu's on her way."

Hazel felt a flood of relief.

"Don't worry, honey. Things'll work out for you."

Hazel accepted Lu's offer and they started a relationship that would last for eight years.

Lu drove all over the midwest for a jobber on the west side of Chicago and was gone for days at a time. Hazel went back to school for her teaching certification and then got a job teaching French. Lu's friends liked Hazel and she and Lu settled into a comfortable routine. They grew to love each other.

Then it happened. The rhythms stopped again. Lu didn't return from her last trip. She'd lost control of the big rig on an icy road in the Ozarks and had gone over a cliff just a few miles from where Hazel had stuck out her thumb eight years before.

For three weeks Hazel listened to their CB radio, hoping to hear Lu's cheerful voice calling to her, "Hey Haze, come in Haze. I'm two miles out on the Ike and coming home!" When Hazel finally shut off the CB, she began walking. She'd leave their apartment two hours before class so she could walk to school. She walked home. On weekends she walked in the park, along the lakefront. She avoided their old friends and talk about Lu by walking for the rest of the term and into the summer. She walked the city's streets, block by block, and in mid-July she passed a former garage that had been converted into something called the Creative Space Center. There was a bright light coming from the door and, on an impulse, Hazel went in.

The light was coming from a welder. Hazel stood listening to the sound of the weld, a sizzling, crackling sound that made her think of the CB static. The light abruptly stopped and the welder raised her mask.

"Hey, you weren't looking at my arc, were ya?"

"I don't know. What's an arc?"

"The light. Didja look at the light? It's dangerous, might burn your eyeballs out."

"Oh. Well, I was only listening to the sound."

The welder smiled at Hazel. "You were listening to the weld, eh? Sounds like bacon frying to me."

Hazel smiled back. There was something about the woman, or maybe it was the welding, that drew her in closer. "Could you teach me to weld?"

"Sure, ain't nothing to it. I'll teach ya, then I'll sell this old machine to ya. Cheap. I'm leaving town in September."

The two women made arrangements to begin the lessons and Hazel walked on home. She had fallen into the habit of talking to Lu in the apartment. "Honey, I'm home," she called as she opened the door. "I found a place over on Clybourn where I can learn welding. I start this Saturday." Hazel wasn't crazy, she knew Lu'd never answer her again, but she just couldn't stop. Not yet.

Hazel liked the welding. She practiced for hours, lost in the noise and clouds of smoke and fumes that surrounded her workbench. Sue, her teacher, seemed amused at Hazel's eagerness. "Hey, slow down girl. This thing ain't going nowhere."

Sue was going somewhere, though. The summer passed quickly and it was time for her to leave.

"Hazel, you gonna buy this thing? I gotta know, 'cause there's a fellow with a garage up on Ashland that's interested."

Hazel paid her and Sue left. Hazel's classes started and she taught during the day and welded at night. For six hours she listened to bored teenagers conjugate French verbs and then she spent four hours at her welding bench. She wasn't making anything special, just laying beads of weld, practicing, hiding within the noise and smoke. She haunted alleys behind factories, collecting scrap metal for her welding and carrying it to the Center in a backpack. A structure was slowly growing beside her workbench. At the end of each welding session she'd take all the smaller parts she'd welded together and weld them to the growing piece. She was trying to get rid of the practice pieces, but they were growing into something unexpected. She'd grasp each one with a pliers, hold it against the structure and weld it on. Her concern was only for physical balance. If the thing seemed about to topple to the left, she'd weld the next piece on the right. Week by week it grew. One crisp night in early November, Hazel was startled to find a carton of steel plates beside her bench. As she looked around the big room, the old man who did woodwork in the back tipped his hat to her.

Hazel walked back to his work area. "Did you put that steel by my bench?"

"Yes." His hair and mustache were gray and his skin was creased, but his eyes were young looking, an unusual light brown color. "I happened onto them and thought of you." He smiled. "I don't know what you're building over there, but maybe you can use the plates."

"Thank you, but really, you shouldn't have gone to the trouble." Hazel was a little uncomfortable. It was the first time she'd paid any attention to the room. It was a large space, divided into work areas. Anybody could rent space there and several projects were scattered around the floor. Hazel felt a twinge of guilt that she hadn't thought to meet the people working around her. She had been too involved with her grief.

"It was no trouble, I have a car." The man was still smiling. "My name's Dan. Daniel Abrams." He held out his hand to her.

"Yes, uh, Dan." Hazel shook his hand. "I'm Hazel Boggs." Then she saw the work on his bench. "Oh. Your carvings are beautiful. The grain glows."

Dan picked up a piece of wood that had bark still on one side. On the other, the natural roughness had been gradually smoothed away, and a face had been carved into it.

"I'm having trouble with this. Each time I pick it up, I see something else trying to get out." He laughed and put it down. "What are you doing over there?"

Hazel shrugged. "Nothing much, mostly just practice. Anyway, thanks for the steel. I'll certainly use it." She returned to her area, picked up a plate from the carton and put it on her bench, opened a new tube of welding rods, kicked on the starter switch and sank back into her cloud.

Each night after that, Dan would wave as she came in. Sometimes there'd be more steel for her and once, there was an exquisitely carved seagull, wings outspread, ready to take off.

"Dan, you can't be giving me this beautiful bird. It must have taken you days to carve it."

"It's that piece you saw before, half bark and half face. I've been watching you while I whittled, and this is what came out of the wood. The face disappeared." Dan raised his eyebrows and laughed. "The inspiration came from you, the bird is you. You must have it."

From then on, Hazel and Dan were friends. By Christmas they'd fallen into the habit of sharing coffee, and by Easter they would meet early, at a restaurant, before going to the Center. On those days, Hazel didn't have time to walk. Although she wasn't aware that she was walking less, it wouldn't have made her stop seeing Dan, even if she had noticed. The man was fun to be around. He told more stories than anyone she'd ever known. Although some of them were so wild that they were hard to believe, they were always entertaining. He had many voices. He could sound like a gangster or a country preacher. Sometimes he'd whisper and sometimes he'd shout. Dan was an entire drama troupe. Hazel listened to him and was glad for his company.

She was getting Dan's life story in serial form. He'd run away from home early in the depression and had spent most of his teen years riding freight trains. He talked of his adventures 'on the rails' as he called it and told of his years in California. He'd worked as a gandy dancer on a railroad section crew, a construction laborer, a car park attendant, and a tuck pointer. He'd been a Baptist deacon, a cotton picker, and a union organizer. Hazel noticed that as he talked, his eyes seemed to focus on the past. His were an old man's memories and they made her remember the old men, potato farmers like her father, who'd gather around a fireplace and talk of the old days when she was a kid. Dan often whittled as he talked, and every once in awhile, another seagull would appear.

One day he handed her one of them. It appeared to be fishing. Its wings were out in a glide position and its head was turned, looking down.

"I don't rightly know why, but this one makes me think of you." Dan said as she took it. "It's looking for something."

Hazel cradled the tiny carving in her hands, her fingers rubbing the smooth grain. "Thanks Dan, it's lovely." She turned it and turned it, looking at it from every angle. "It makes me think of a seagull I used to feed." She told Dan about the bird and how it would sometimes glide along beside her as she rode her bike, begging for food or attention, its head turned just as the carved bird's was. It was the first time she'd talked about herself to Dan.

"How'd you get to Chicago?" He asked. "It's really a long way."

Although reluctant at first, she gradually warmed to talking about her past and she shared stories with Dan as the summer progressed. He whittled as they talked and more gulls appeared.

Hazel's favorite stories were from Dan's days as a hobo. One day he told her about jumping off a railroad bridge into the Mississippi River because a train was bearing down on him as he crossed the bridge. It was in January and the water was icy cold. Somehow he'd survived the shock and made it to the shore.

"Oh Dan, that's too hard to believe. How could you have survived the fall? The shock of hitting that icy water should have stunned you and you'd have drowned."

"I don't pretend to know why I made it, only that I did. Maybe it was like the time when I was a kid and my brothers threw me into the bayou to teach me to swim. I sank straight down. When I hit bottom, I opened my eyes and saw a big old alligator gar looking right at me. Did you ever see a gar, Hazel? They have a mouth full of teeth. I levitated! I rose above the surface of that bayou, my arms and legs achurning, and I practically walked on the water to get out of there." Dan's eyes flashed and his arms churned the air as he spoke. "Anyway, I did make it to the shore, washed up on the snowy bank, half frozen. I'd probably have died right there if an old country preacher hadn't found me. He took me home and he and his wife stripped me down and rubbed goose grease all over my body." Dan's hands rested. "It was the goose grease that saved me from pneumonia, or so they said. Even today, when I smell that stuff, I think of them."

"What's goose grease smell like?"

"Bad. It smells bad."

Hazel laughed. "But Dan, I still can't believe you could have made it through all that."

"Look, Hazel, if I tell you the chicken chews tobacco, you know you can look under her left wing and find a tin of W. E. Garret." Dan always swore to the truth of his stories. "But that's only if I tell you that, 'cause I don't lie."

"What's W. E. Garrett?"

"It's a tobacco company. Chewing tobacco and snuff. How did you get to be this old without knowing that?" Dan leaned forward and cocked an eyebrow.

Hazel laughed. Dan really was a lot of fun. The summer passed and his stories continued. Whenever she doubted him, he would remind her of the chicken.

School started again and Hazel settled into her old routine of welding after class. She and Dan would talk as they left the Center and he'd often give her a ride home. She hardly ever walked anymore. The welded structure beside her bench was about six feet tall and it extended outward in twisting arms of steel. Hazel could no longer reach the top, so the thing was starting to grow downward, toward its beginning.

Dan became ill. He had pneumonia, he told her when he called from the hospital. She went to visit him, taking some goose grease she'd gotten from a butcher. It was three months before Dan was strong enough to resume his wood carvings at the Center. He was amazed at the change in her welding.

"What's it becoming, Hazel?" Dan asked as he walked around it. "It's gone up as far as it can go and then it came back down again. It's circled around, spread out, returned, and now it's on the way back up."

While he was away, Hazel'd bought a grinder and had polished what old welds she could reach and all of the new ones. It was raw, unfinished on the inside, polished on the outside.

"I like it," he said.

During his illness, Hazel had often thought of his stories and she'd especially remembered the chicken. Dan had told her a lot about himself. He'd talked about the pain of being a kid alone in an adult world, but he'd made it funny. His pain had become humor and an ability to see beyond the immediate crisis. If something worked, it became a truth. Lu had been like that. She'd accepted Hazel, dirty from

her garden, without questions. Lu's easy humor had
made the space Hazel needed. Now Dan was doing
the same thing. Hazel looked at his creased face and
she remembered reading somewhere that a person
wears God's face until he is about thirty. What he
looks like after that is his own fault. She'd come to
love the lines of Dan's face, lines that folded easily
around his smiles and outlined his light brown eyes.
She had loved Lu's face, too. A face that had meant
she would survive. Hazel started to talk about Lu.

"I loved her, Dan. It wasn't easy at first, you know,
to love another woman. She let me take my time and
one day, while she was on the road, I realized I
missed her. I missed seeing her face across the
breakfast table. I missed hearing her laugh. I missed
talking to her. I was in love and hadn't even realized
it." She sighed. "Lu was a wonderful lover." Lu had
made Hazel feel like all the currents of Lake
Michigan were flowing right through her. Hazel
couldn't go on for a few moments. Finally, in a small
voice, "Dan, I miss her so."

She looked at him and saw that his arms were
open and she walked into them and cried against his
chest. When she finally calmed, she drew away
self-consciously.

"It's there, Hazel." Dan touched her arm and
turned her toward the welded structure. "Look
inside it. The welds are rough, the pieces stuck
together any which way. Later you started putting
balance, you began to even things out, the welds got
smoother. Finally you turned it back from its flight
and brought it down, connected it to itself and
polished away the seams." Dan's calloused hands
were moving over the sculpture as he spoke. "You

welded your pain, Hazel. You'll never be without Lu because she's a part of you now. It's all here."

"I used to clutch the electrode cable between my legs as I welded so I could feel the power surging through it. I needed that quiver, the noise, and the smoke."

"And I caress the wood as I polish it. I need to feel it come alive again."

That night, when Dan dropped her off at her apartment, Hazel unlocked the door and went quietly in. She sat at her desk and corrected papers until she felt drowsy, then she made a cup of tea and drank it. She took a shower and then began walking around the apartment, looking at the clutter of ten years on one place. Lu's things were still everywhere. The CB sat, dusty now, on the back of a counter in the kitchen. Lu had been fond of the arts of mountain women, and the craftwork she'd bought on her trips decorated the apartment. Hazed refolded a handsewn quilt at the end of the sofa. She touched the tiny embroidered stitches on a pillow. She repositioned three cornhusk dolls that shared an end table with Dan's seagulls. Then she crossed the room, went down the hall and into the bedroom. She opened a closet and got out one of Lu's nightgowns; it had hand tatted lace across the bodice. Quickly stripping off her own, she dropped Lu's gown over head. As it slid down her body, she could feel the tension of her muscles easing. Suddenly tired, she turned back the quilt on the bed and lay down. She shut off the light. Turning over, she pulled the quilt around her shoulders and with her fingers feeling the lace she'd so often felt over Lu's breasts, she whispered, "Good night, Lu."

Paul Hoover

Demonstration

It was 1969, and I had six months to go as a conscientious objector at Memorial Hospital in Chicago. Norman Morrison, the Quaker, had set himself on fire outside the Pentagon, and the word "immolation" entered the national vocabulary. It was my job to ask patients about the condition of their mashed potatoes, supervise the station clerks, and, since there were no transportation aides on the evening shift, take bodies to the morgue. Luckily, morgue time wasn't a major part of the job; most nights I watched Johnny Carson on a patient's TV. Once, a bunch of us crowded into a room in Orthopedics and saw Tiny Tim marry Miss Vicki, but it wasn't as funny as everyone had expected. Johnny himself took it all very seriously, and there was uneasiness in the room.

Two revolutionaries, Carlo and Edgar, had just moved into our apartment on Halsted Street. My other roommates, Steve and Lowe, were both 4-F, Steve because of his four-foot-eleven stature and Lowe because of his drug-induced visions. According to the Army psychologist, there was so much residual LSD in his system you could start a car with him if you had the right kind of cables. His obsession with locking the door had already rubbed off on Carlo, who had been in prison for defacing draft records with ketchup. When Lowe went into one of his lengthy inspections—locking, unlocking, relocking—Carlo would assist, standing outside in the hall, turning the knob, and shouting through the

door. Edgar spent much of his time at a portable
typewriter, working on political tracts he signed
"Cyclops," but in the evening and on Saturday
morning he'd be more sociable, watching TV with
Steve and Lowe. Since he'd become a revolutionary,
Edgar said, he hadn't had time for television.
Moreover, it was the primary tool of capitalist
education. When he watched Steve's favorite shows,
he did so as a scholar, analyzing the politics of
Bullwinkle and Bugs Bunny.

Steve differed in the matter of Bugs. Wasn't it true,
as the French Surrealists believed, that Bugs Bunny
was an anarchic hero of the Left? His outrageous
behavior symbolized revolutionary youth, the mad
and dispossessed, while Elmer Fudd was the
bourgeois ideal of militarism (Fudd as hunter),
imperialism (Fudd evicts Bugs from his home), and
the leisure class (Fudd has no discernible job).

Edgar thought about that. While Steve had a point
about Fudd, Bugs Bunny was also a landholder, in
spite of the "underground" metaphor of his living
conditions. And his frequent recognition of audience,
by winking or waving, was a formalist gesture
characteristic of the most retrograde anti-socialist
and decadent phases of modern Russian art. Bugs as
"avant-garde" on the surface, but his embracement
of the paying audience was no different from that of
a butcher shaking a pork chop in a housewife's face.

Steve scowled and worked his small hands
together. He believed in the anti-authoritarian stance
of cartoon characters, most of whom conspired with
the youthful audience to subvert parental authority.
If Bugs Bunny were co-opted by the status quo, then
revolution would in a sense be impossible,
opposition reduced to an adolescent gesture, to be

outgrown as one entered adult society. Children understood better than their parents what it was to be free, and they must eventually teach their anarchism to the Fudds.

Edgar thought Steve was a revolutionary simpleton. Steve had to understand that the whole medium of television was empowered by capitalism. It was saturated with the values of that system, and reiterated them. Weren't there commercials for toys and cereal between the cartoons? What about the violence? Capitalist technology was designed as a hymn to itself, and it included movies and television.

"Not books?" I asked from the dining room.

"Certainly not," said Edgar, "because there the technology is so archaic it's roughly equivalent to speech, which is free. Virtually anybody can get his hands on a printing press."

"But the education that shapes that speech isn't free," I said. "What school did you go to?"

"Princeton," he said.

"Franklin College," I said, pointing to my chest.

"Never heard of it."

"There you go," I said.

"It proves nothing," Edgar replied.

We argued for a while about the relative value of our educations, and I asked Edgar how he made a living.

The question caught him off guard, and his eyes narrowed. "I can't talk about that," he said.

"Because you get your money from home?" I asked.

"No!" he said. "At least not at the present time."

"Tell the man where you get your bread," Carlo said to Edgar, looking at me with yellow eyes.

"I did get a certain amount from my trust fund," Edgar said, "but that is no longer necessary. Now I have my own income, earned through my own efforts." He seemed very proud of his abilities as a wage earner, yet I'd never seen him go to work.

"But what do you do, exactly?" I asked.

Edgar looked around the room, and Carlo nodded O.K. "Actually," Edgar said, "I go around the world cashing stolen traveller's checks. I get them from an associate who works hand in hand with the owner of the checks. The owner buys ten thousand dollars' worth in large denominations, gives them to my friend, then goes to American Express and claims they're missing. They give him replacements, but meanwhile I travel from London to Amsterdam to Paris, cashing the checks as fast as I can. I go only to the largest banks, where the size of the checks will prove no problem."

"You got to work fast," said Carlo, "before the list gets around."

"They compile a list of missing checks," said Edgar, "so all transactions must be complete within two days. Of course, the original owner gets a share, and my associate and I split the rest."

"Aren't you afraid of getting caught?" asked Lowe, in awe of Edgar's life of adventure.

"There is some risk involved," Edgar said coolly," but the rewards are very good. There was a real problem on only one occasion."

"Dallas," said Carlo, laughing to himself.

"I was scheduled to receive the checks directly from the owner, whose name was Howdy Brown, but when he showed up he was already being chased by the state police. He picked me up in front of a suburban motel in his blue Cadillac convertible and

we took off at a hundred miles an hour. We were a
few miles down the road, heading into the desert,
when I heard the siren. It was pretty far behind us,
but getting closer. None of this concerned Howdy
Brown in the least. He was a big red-faced cowboy,
and he made normal conversation about football and
the weather before pulling the checks out of his
jacket."

"Tell 'em about the baby," Carlo said, gesturing
with a quart of beer.

"The craziest part was Howdy Brown's little boy.
He'd been sitting in back the whole time, playing
with some toys, but when the cops got nearer
Howdy thought he would have some fun. He yelled
at the kid, whose name was Goober, to come up
front. Goober had blond hair and couldn't have been
more than two. He was still wearing a diaper. But he
climbed over the back of the seat, which is difficult
at that speed, and stood at the steering wheel.
Howdy sat in the middle with his foot on the gas,
and Goober held the wheel with both hands. He was
jumping up and down with excitement. The wind
blew his face so hard it made him look Chinese. He
was an excellent driver. Most of the road was dead
straight ahead; he kept us right in the middle, so we
cut the white line right through the hood ornament.
When a car came from the other direction, he'd ease
the Cadillac over into the right lane with no
problem. Evidently he'd done this kind of driving
before."

Carlo loved the story, even though he'd heard it
many times. So did Steve, who'd forgotten his
philosophical differences with Edgar. Lowe seemed
to regard Edgar as a celebrity.

"So what happened?" I said. "Did you get away from the cops?"

"It was a supercharged engine, according to Howdy. They were chasing him on a speeding violation. He let them pull up next to us, laughed at their reaction to the baby driver, and floored it. The cops didn't have a chance against us."

About this time, we decided to go down to the Loop for a demonstration against the war. We hated the war, we especially hated the government, but most of all we hated L.B.J.'s showing his surgical scar to the nation. It was all right if your uncle did it, between the fourth and fifth beer, but the President wasn't allowed. The demonstration was to take place on State Street, in the heart of the shopping district. Carlo and Edgar had something to do with it, indirectly, though the Union for a Free Union, a radical-leftist group. Steve went with them, and Lowe and I planned to meet them later. Around noon we climbed the subway stairs into warm sunlight. A large crowd looked on from the sidewalks—office workers on their lunch breaks. A smaller group of about two hundred white college students sat in the middle of the street, like a senior-class picnic.

Lowe had been smoking joints all morning in preparation for the event, but grass had begun to make me nervous, so I was laying off. He talked softly to himself in a rhythmic fashion, as he often did—a list of the states and their capitals in alphabetical order. He was up to South Dakota. I told him I'd always liked the sound of "Helena, Montana."

We had expected a stage and microphone, some minimal preparations, but there was nothing. The stage was the street. The idea was to stop traffic, and it had worked. Buses and cars were lined up to the south and north as far as you could see. At the edge of the crowd, two buses were side by side, with their doors open; the drivers leaned on their steering wheels, watching the demonstrators through the enormous windshields. They seemed in no hurry. The faces I saw through the windows were all black. Some looked restlessly down at the crowd, but most were reading or staring into space. The sky was a perfect blue, a shade you see only in Chicago, or maybe Oslo. A couple of pigeons struggled over the crowd, as if inconvenienced.

I saw Steve sitting on the curb across the street. He had half entered the demonstration, like a bather testing the water. I didn't see Carlo, but Edgar was at the rear of the crowd on the other side, taking pictures of the F.B.I. with a small camera. Poorly disguised as students, they walked blatantly among the seated demonstrators, taking their pictures. Two agents pointed to each other, indicating a sector of students that had been missed. I wondered what kind of files they must have, to go to this kind of trouble.

The crowd began to stir as the agents moved through. One of them must have stepped on someone, because a young guy with brown hair and a denim jacket shoved the agent from a sitting position. The agent shoved him back, and suddenly the crowd began to writhe, like planarias around a particle of food. Some of the demonstrators stood, trying to calm things down, but it didn't work. The guy in the denim jacket, possibly a provocateur, leaped on the agent's back, and the whole street went up for grabs. The agent swung around in anger and threw him over his shoulder onto a group of women.

One of them screamed and held her face, and blood ran between her fingers. A few Chicago cops, who had been standing at the edge of the crowd trying not to call attention to themselves, waded into the street with clubs, knocking people aside. Most of the demonstrators jumped to their feet and danced away from the blows, but a few more stalwart types linked arms and stayed put. It was a classic nonviolent position to take but the cops hadn't read Gandhi. They laid into the group with the ends of their sticks. People ran and screamed; Edgar spun this way and that, recording fragments of chaos. The two bus drivers had closed their doors and dropped out of sight. Passengers were looking at the street with horror; one elderly black man screamed something we couldn't hear.

Lowe and I leaned against the building behind us, amazed at the swiftness of events and unable to run. A few squadrols pulled up on Jackson, and about fifty cops wearing riot gear marched around the corner, holding extra-long clubs ahead of them like flagpoles, one end braced on the stomach. The first row was especially impressive—tall and heavy, with faces like bulldogs'. By now the street was mostly deserted, but the sidewalk was swarming. The cops had dragged off a lot of demonstrators and pushed them into squadrols. The riot squad spread out to sweep the street, creating a rush of onlookers in our direction. Clinging to the building didn't work. Somebody knocked into me with tremendous force, and I fell into Lowe. We went down on the sidewalk, pressed against each other. Somebody stepped on my back, then several people fell on us. Lowe pushed me in the face with both hands, as if I was smothering him, and somehow I got to my feet and started

running. It must have been in the wrong direction,
because there was a stinging blur. I couldn't see or
hear anymore. I was lying on the sidewalk in a pool
of blood, and I was dead to the world.

Mistakes get made at the hospital, no doubt about
it. There's a test they give to find the site of a spinal
injury. The doctor injects a radiopaque dye into the
spinal column, puts the patient on an X-ray table,
and tilts the table to make the dye run up or down.
He watches the travelling dye bump along the
column, and the beauty of medicine is never more
clear. When the dye reaches the injury, it stops or
spreads, and the doctor makes a note on the chart.
One the day Dr. Wing performed the test on Johnny
Matthews, a twelve-year-old quadriplegic who'd
been struck by a stray bullet on New Year's Eve,
things didn't go so well. The story was that the
doctor forgot what he was doing and allowed the
dye to flow all the way to the brain. This caused a
respiratory arrest, and the boy died on the table.
Wing covered his tracks by shading the history and
progress notes, and no one in the family was astute
enough to sue, but the nurses knew what had
happened. When Wing sat down with them in the
employee dining room, they'd leave or sit in icy
silence.

That's why when I woke up in the neurological
unit and Dr. Wing was looking into my eyes, I was a
little concerned. His cold finger lifted an eyelid while
he shined a light in there.

"I think he's awake," he said to the nurse. It was
Eileen Bass, from the day shift.

There was an I.V. in my right arm, and the bed rail
on the other side was up. There was also a tightness

in my left arm, which I realized was a restraint. This
was quite a surprise, since restraints are usually
applied only when the patient is out of his mind.

"Nagloo," I said.

The doctor stood back from the bed in an attitude
of caution, but Eileen came close to look at me.

"Why, he's all right," she said. "He's trying to say
something is all." She lifted off the small green
oxygen mask and rubbed my cheeks to get the red
marks out. It must have been on for some time,
because the skin felt numb. "Are you all right, hon?"
she said, giving me a pat.

"Fine," I said. "What happened?"

"We had to tie you down," she said. "You were
pulling out the I.V."

"I don't remember."

Wing took her place as she went to the other side
and straightened the covers. "We put you on the
intravenous basically for feeding," he said. "We
didn't know how long you'd be out. We'll start you
on a liquid diet at lunch and see how you tolerate
it."

"Can you take off the restraint, please? It's hurting
my arm."

"Are you sure you're feeling O.K.?" he said in a
patronizing tone. "You didn't behave very well last
night."

"I promise to behave."

"That's a good boy," he said, patting me on the
head. He waved his hand, and Eileen started untying
the restraint.

"You've had a concussion," said Wing, pushing on
the bridge of his glasses. "We're going to do some
tests, but if everything works out you can think
about going home in a couple of days."

"What kind of tests?"

"Brain scan, skull X-rays, and EEG."

"You think I've got a fracture?"

"We'll see."

He looked as if he'd been on duty for a day and a half already. His clothes were wrinkled and his face sagged. Yawning broadly, he rubbed his hand through the thick black hair that was matted here and sticking out there.

"What time is it?" I asked.

"Nine in the morning," said Eileen, struggling with the final knot.

"So I've been here since yesterday afternoon?"

"That's right," said Wing, looking at his watch.

Eileen got the restraint off, and I lifted the arm to get blood into it. The shoulder was a little sore.

Wing looked into my eyes again with the penlight, as if frowning at the back of a cave, then held up four fingers and asked me how many there were. Pulling down the sheet, he stuck a little pin into the soles of my feet to see if there was feeling. There was. Then he ran his fingernail the length of the sole, from heel to toe, to see which way the toes would curl. If they curled down, it meant you were O.K., and if they curled back toward your face, you were brain-damaged or something. I was not brain-damaged, but I had a huge ache where the head met the spinal column. I pointed to where it hurt, and Wing frowned.

"Not good?" I asked.

"Could be a subdural hematoma. Some people can walk around for a week with one, then they drop dead from it, just like that." He snapped his fingers with finality. It's just like a time bomb, a walking time bomb."

"That's reassuring," I said.

"Usually it's a sign if one eye dilates more than the other."

"What should I do—carry a mirror?"

He was one of those guys who had worked so hard ever since med school he couldn't tell if you were kidding.

"That wouldn't be very practical, would it?" he said.

"Subdurals can be tricky," said Eileen.

A tall kid wearing a white interne's jacket walked in. He had blond hair that fell over one eye, and his pink hands were huge.

"Walters!" said Wing. "Just the man I wanted to see."

"Is this the patient? Walters was looking at Eileen, not me.

"Yes," said Wing. "I want you to take him to EEG, but first do a full workup."

"O.K.," said Walters, with no enthusiasm. He acted as if he wanted to be outside playing basketball with the other kids.

"Walters here is your doctor," Wing said. "I'm just supervising. Then, as if Walters weren't there, he said, "He looks young, but he's brilliant. Best scores on the state boards in thirty-seven years." He left, taking Eileen with him.

Walters didn't have much to say. As he did another workup, he sighed a lot and looked out the window. But he seemed to know what he was doing, which was exactly what Wing had done. If I wasn't mistaken, my toes curled the opposite direction this time, but he didn't say anything. He looked very sad and disconcerted.

"Is something wrong?" I asked.

"I was just thinking about home," he said.

"I guess you're on a pretty fast track."

"Pretty fast." He sighed. "Dad thinks it's not fast enough."

"You're not from Chicago, are you?"

"Elwood, Illinois. Downstate."

"Are you going back there to practice?"

"Got to. The Chamber of Commerce is paying my tuition."

"You have a contract with them?"

"I have to take up with Dr. Simmons, who's about to retire, and stay in town for at least five years."

"Do you want to do that?"

"Oh, sure," he said morosely. He went to look for a cart to take me down to EEG.

There was coughing on the other side of the curtain. I'd thought I was alone.

"Hello?" I said.

"Hi!"

"I didn't realize I had a roommate."

"The name's Feller," he said. "Arnold Feller." His voice sounded muffled, as if it passed through two or three doors.

"Any relation to Bob?"

"Who's that?" he asked softly.

"Baseball player, one of the greats."

"I don't follow sports," he said.

"My name is Holder. Jim Holder."

"Pleased to meet you."

"I got hit on the head at a demonstration," I said.

"What were you demonstrating?" he asked, with great labor.

I realized he thought I meant a Ronco vegetable slicer or something.

"You sound like you're in pain," I said. "Maybe we should talk later."

"That's all right. I like to talk."

"Too bad I can't reach the curtain."

"Me neither," he said.

A suction pump engaged on his side, a little motor sounded like someone's fingers tapping on a table. He must have had surgery, since the pump, called a Gumco, is used to drain a wound.

"I don't see a TV in the room," I complained.

"It's over here, up on the wall. I'm watching Captain Cartoon."

"I don't hear anything."

"With these shows you don't need sound," he said.

"The doctor says I might have a subdural."

There was no answer for a while. Then he said, "What did you say?"

"I might have a subdural," I said much louder, as if calling over a wall. A bruise on my brain."

There was another long pause.

"It can knock you over any time," I said, snapping my fingers. "Just like that."

I thought I could hear, very distantly, the frantic sounds of cartoon mice pounding each other with clubs. After a while his suction pump went silent.

"You there?" he said.

"Yeah."

"Just checking."

Walters wheeled in a cart, but its pad was missing, which filled me with horror. Somebody must have recently used it to take a body to the morgue.

"There's no pad," I said. "It's got to have a pad."

"I had a hard time finding this one," he whined.

"Where did you get it?"

"Back by the elevators."

"Look in the stationary closet around the corner from there."

"Doggone it," he said, as if complaining to one of his parents.

We got off the elevator on the third floor and wheeled down the hall, Walters' long head over me like a horse's. At the very end, there was a door that was painted red instead of stained and varnished. A plaque on it said "EEG" and under that "DEATH STUDIES."

"Wait a minute," I said. "What's death studies?"

"It's the same as EEG," he said, opening the door, "only we do it to see if you're dead."

Death Studies was a small windowless room, about the size of a Buick Electra. Walters could barely fit the cart inside. I had to stand in the hallway in my patient gown, then climb back onto the cart once he'd wedged it in. Next to me was a large gray machine with dozens of lights and electrodes and a wide strip of gray paper under several dormant styluses. There was no technician, just a chair for Walters to sit on. It took quite a while to get me hooked up, since electrodes had to be placed all around my head.

As the machine jerked to a start, the styluses flipping like crab claws, I remembered one of the C.O. jobs I'd seen advertised. Every evening, at some university lab in New Jersey, they would hook you up to one of these machines. While you slept, it registered changes in your brain waves. They could tell if you were restless and if you were happy. They could even tell if you were in a creative state and if you had a reptile mind. It was rumored to be hard duty, however. One C.O. reported that the loss of privacy he'd endured during sleep studies had made him nearly crazy. Something wasn't right about sleeping under the gaze of a technician marking things on a clipboard. He said he aged ten years in six weeks.

I had no such problems. For some reason I was very relaxed, like a puppy curled up with a ticking clock. All sorts of things came into my head: a math grade I got in school, the weatherman on Channel 5 pointing at a bolt of lightning on a fuzzy map. Walters spoke in a bored voice punctuated by sighs, and one of the things he said was "It says here you're asleep."

The next day, Dr. Wing signed me out of the hospital. He came into the room in a hurry and started to shoo me out, using his hands like brooms.

"Go, go—you're fine," he said. "I've got to get busy here. We need this bed for a myasthenia gravis that's coming this afternoon." Myasthenia is a disease that causes its victims to lose control of their muscles. After a while, they even lose the strength to open their eyes, and soon they are too weak to breath. But the disease couldn't have gone too far if the patient taking my place wasn't in Intensive Care.

Steve, Lowe, and Carlo came to pick me up. The curving imprint of a boot sole ran across Steve's black-and-blue cheek. He sat next to the curtain, listening to the sounds of "Jeopardy" from Arnold Feller's TV. Lowe seemed fine. He hadn't been injured, though he mumbled more than usual, and his fascination with a green plastic water pitcher was approaching a trance. Carlo, who wore Edgar's old Nehru jacket and talked in prison whispers, said he had caught the whole thing from the roof of a building where he was stationed with a camera to record police brutality. He'd seen Edgar running down State Street, holding the hand of a girl Carlo didn't know. Edgar and the girl had jumped into a yellow Porsche and sped away, and hadn't been heard from since.

Carlo showed me the shots from his Kodak Instamatic. He hadn't realized he'd need a telescopic lens; they looked like embroidered rugs.

Getting What You Came For

She was a fool then. "You a FOOL!" Dima had said. "A FOOL to go there!" She kept hearing the ripping of pages from the textbook. Paula needed to walk today, to think. She went to the White Hen, bought milk and tape.

She was a fool to walk here, too. Oh, the city had good intentions, as it always had, despite its corrupt leaders, for the forty years she'd lived in it. They built sidewalks without curbs so the seniors could move their grocery carts and wheelchairs more easily up and down Sheridan Road. But now all these young cyclists from Rogers Park and from these very condo buildings ignored the bike paths, ignored the warnings painted on the sidewalk as they rode over them: *No bicycles on sidewalk.* Red letters on a shiny white background.

Sylvia wouldn't have let them bother her. She'd be riding her bike on the Kenmore path, her long black hair wrapped in a bun, her red windbreaker flapping around her thick, strong torso. Sylvia had ridden the winds to Seattle eleven years ago for a job offer she couldn't turn down. Paula stayed on, typing and filing for the same Loop firm she retired from last year. Afraid to leave, to go where she wanted.

As she reached her building, a white ambulance drew up just ahead. It stopped just across the street, flashing its red light. A police car pulled up, and a young male cyclist stood, unhurt, apparently trying to defend himself. Then the paramedics came around the van and wheeled the stretcher out. They

disappeared on the other side for a few minutes, and
when Paula saw them again a form about the size of
Mrs. Shyamhari's lay on it. She was covered halfway
with the sheet, but as they lifted her up, Mrs.
Shyamhari's long, dark braid flopped over the edge.

"I KNEW something like this would happen,"
Mrs. Goldstein was telling Mike, a tall, muscular
Pole, their building super. "I KNEW somebody was
going to get hurt. I tell you, you're taking your life in
your hands when you walk out the door."

"Yes, ma'am," Mike said and turned back to
preparing the spring flowerbeds.

Mrs. Goldstein always seemed angry, as if she'd
spent a lifetime of effort and still hadn't
accomplished whatever it was she'd set out to do.

Inside, Paula picked up the mail from companies
that wanted her business and charities and political
groups that wanted her donations. On the seventh
floor, in her small apartment, she put away the milk.
Then she washed her hands and dried them, as she
always did after going out, and vigorously rubbed
them with lotion.

She sat at the walnut table that had been Sylvia's.
As carefully as though she were lifting pressed
butterfly wings, she laid the torn pages precisely next
to each other. The tape went on smooth and sure.
She pressed down with her thumbnail and drew it all
the way down the crease, making the seal firm. Then
she went to the next set of pages and repeated the
process. And again.

Kniga kak novaya! she thought. The book is as
good as new.

But the man, Dima: would he be as good as new?
Her only friend in the building, besides Mrs.
Shyamhari. He was teaching her Russian. He tried so

hard not to lose his temper, and when he did, he always tortured himself, pained by a remorse greater than she'd ever seen in a man. He suffered for days afterward, like a child obsessed. Sometimes she let him stew. Sometimes she sought him out, took him a loaf of fresh zucchini bread. But this time, she hardly knew what to do. Never before had he done something destructive. And against the language, no less. Like striking his own mother.

She'd have to give him a day or two. "Why go THERE!" he had suddenly shouted. "So many nice places to go, why all of sudden you go there?! It is not necessary. By the way, it is not a very pleasant place, and your money only helps the government. KGB will spy on you. Here, you have me. Ask any question. I will tell you."

But she could not tell him why, just as she knew he would never let her know how desperately he longed to return for a visit. Probably he could not even let himself know how much he wished it. She wanted to go. For Sylvia. Though it was too late.

Finally, she had gone to Seattle, to help, when Sylvia had told her about the cancer. Sylvia died seven years after leaving Chicago, three years before Paula retired and might have joined her.

And now she was going to travel at last to Russia and the Far East. When the tour stopped in Odessa, Paula would look for the streets where Sylvia began. Sylvia's father had moved the family when she was eight. None of them had ever gone back. Sylvia had planned to go with Paula, but then there wasn't time. They had talked of it, sporadically, for years. Now Paula would go alone. Why not?

But Dima, as the date approached, could hardly bear to hear her mention it. "How can you go and leave us here, the lake going to eat us all up and you not even in country!" A few weeks ago winter storms had blown waves against the condos across the street. The half block of Rosemont from Sheridan to Lake Michigan was covered with water up to the windows of cars. A few tenants had to leave their apartments for weeks, and the damage to buildings and roads and cars was a million dollars.

Maybe Dima was right. Today, almost safely into spring, she watched the lake from her window. The lake was coming for all of this property, sooner or later. Like the city, the developers had good intentions when they dredged and filled all the way from Broadway over to where Sheridan was now. Made new neighborhoods where before there was water. For nearly a lifetime it had lasted. How much longer? Dima said things were fine until they built the high-rises east of Sheridan. If they'd left just a few yards, a few feet where concrete did not intrude on the water, the lake might have let them be. Now that same concrete and brick gave the water nowhere to go, and it had to dig under them. One day she'd look out her window just like this and watch the high-rise just south of her at Granville fall into the waves.

Dima worried enough for everyone. She hardly needed to. Why worry about Dima? Why go to his door? Better to see about Mrs. Shyamhari.

On the 151 bus there were many empty seats. Two other ladies sat up front and a young couple in the back. Paula sat in relative peace until a skinny man with an angry frown got on and took the seat across the aisle. He began watching her as though he wanted something. Should she move to an empty seat? No one else noticed him. What was it that made some young people so aggressive, so eager to hurt others? Or bitter? This young man, for example. Something had to have made him hate people, something had to have made him so insensitive to her need to be left alone.

She wished he would get off the bus.

As the bus neared the stop near the hospital, he was still staring at her. As she got up, clutching her canvas satchel, he sneered.

"You ugly, lady."

The words were loud enough for everyone to hear. Her ears hurt as if he had put up a megaphone against her head. She got to the exit door and down the steps. The bus stopped. The doors opened at last.

"You ugly, and you OLD. Real old. Good ridd-ANCE, lady. Get out my face and get yo' ass off the street."

The words followed her. How dare he! What had she ever done to him or to anyone he knew? Nothing. Tears started to come, but she wouldn't let them. Other women had suffered far worse than she at the hands of young men like him. All over the city they'd been attacked, robbed, beaten, raped, and killed.

Nobody got off easy here. Nobody could escape. Those groups of young men would get you, or the cyclists would get you, or eventually the lake would get you; it didn't matter. A woman who didn't die young was a forbidden thing. Taboo. Hardly a week went by when she didn't see a bag lady on a bus bench, her face coarsened beyond anyone's recognition.

She reached the hospital entrance. Some got what they came for. The burglars who broke into the laundry room three times in the last year. The rapist released from prison who raped five more on the North side a month after he was out.

People coming after other people. And people losing what they thought they came for too. Several ladies her age and older in her building had families. Husbands lost to heart attacks, grown children to jobs in other cities. Paula had never married, never raised a family, but now nothing separated her from the other women. None of them ever knew about Sylvia. What did it matter now? Like poor Mrs. Goldstein. Alone despite a family. Her kids got away as quick as they could. Couldn't take all that clutching and controlling. People got themselves trained, somehow, to invade other people. Hurt or help—didn't much matter. Still invasion.

Maybe by coming here she was the same. It was so easy to think you were doing the right thing and to mess it up anyway.

The shiny greenish-gray paint and the smooth tile floors gave off no warmth. Patients were wheeled from emergency to x-ray back to emergency. Doctors were perpetually addressed over loudspeakers, visitors referred to other desks, other nurses, no one seeming to know when all this chaos would end.

Paula asked at the right desk, did as she was told, sat and waited, watching the doorway Mrs. Shyamhari would be coming through. Mrs. Shyamhari would not require hospitalization. She had cuts and bruises; unfortunately, one of the cuts was deep, right on the knee, where the stitches would pull out easily, and she would have to use crutches at first.

The bus would never do. Mrs. Shyamhari would also be worried about getting her daughter from school and getting to the restaurant on time. It was already past two o'clock. They could take a cab; Paula could pay the fare. But Mrs. Shyamhari probably wouldn't let her.

The pay telephone was just outside the door. Paula punched in the numbers slowly and deliberately.

"Yah, I know. Mike already told me when I got mail. Why you go alone? You know I take you. You wait. I come now and pick you up. We take her home in car."

She was glad to see Mrs. Shyamhari hobble in before Dima arrived. "Mrs. Paula! You should not have come!"

"Of course I should." She helped Mrs. Shyamhari through the exit doors. They waited on the sidewalk until Dima drove up.

"So sorry to be of trouble," Mrs. Shyamhari told Dima as they helped her into the old maroon sedan.

"Is no trouble," Dima admonished her. "Young hooligans is trouble. Hitting lady on sidewalk in daylight!"

"That's right, Mrs. Shyamhari. Everyone is upset about those cyclists. Maybe now the alderman can get the city council to listen."

"They should ride on Kenmore and Winthrop, where they belong," Dima said. "If the police don't arrest them, I'll tell them something. Anytime you need a ride, you just let Dima know. 505. You come to me. I take you to get little girl. I take you where you need."

Listening to Dima was like sliding into a warm bath and letting all her muscles of resistance go slack. Dima was happy to be helping Mrs. Shyamhari; Mrs. Shyamhari reluctantly allowed him and was duly grateful, and she, Paula, could let things go on just as they were. Like the snow. In Russian, the snow *goes*. It just goes.

"We have a lesson this afternoon, o.k.?" he asked her the next morning as they sat in the lobby, watching the mail carrier sorting.

No sign of nervousness. Maybe he really was all right.

She brought the repaired book. He winced when he saw it, but said nothing. He offered her tea, coffee.

"Or maybe vodka? You get ready for trip? In your hotel, you watch, they give you vodka every night. Keep you happy. Keep you not see things."

She ignored him. Older emigres like Dima were immune to the promise of *glasnost*. She asked for tea.

"Now, answer me." In Russian, he asked her how many children she had.

She managed the Russian answer. "*Oo menya nyet detei.*"

They continued, with question-and-answers for directions, expressions of sympathy, gratitude, hunger, cold, and discomfort.

Suddenly, Dima stopped.

"And what will they say when they look at you, not believing you never married, not believing you have no children?!"

She stared and put her teacup down. Dima had never addressed her about this. She had felt somehow safe with him as her friendly but respectful neighbor. She had moved into the building after Sylvia left the city. Many people her age lived alone. Dima had never pressured her to talk about her life. And now it seemed so many years ago, in another

life, that she had her love. It was no one's business,
not even Dima's.

"They will demand to know," he continued.
"They will say, but WHY?! Why you have no
children? They will not believe you. Especially the
Georgians and the Ukrainians."

"Then they'll just have to doubt me, Dima."

"Ha? You think it will be easy? You think you will
have nice hot water, nice comfort, like you do here?
You think you will sleep well? Sure you will, in the
foreign hotels."

"Dima, we've been through this before. Maybe I
should go."

She stood up.

"Sure. You go. You leave old Dima alone. Why
you go there to have fat old Russians make love to
you? You forget how loyal your Dima is! And I right
here and you don't even see me!"

Later, she thought about his words. Had she truly
never seen that he wanted more from her? Had she
been blind to him? Not to see that their mutual
affection meant more to him, left him longing?
Suddenly she felt both sadness and gratitude that
someone, at least, found her not ugly, but desirable
still. Perhaps she owed him more after all.

But then she heard the memory of Sylvia's sharp
voice inside her head, when Paula wouldn't ask for a
raise at Litchfield and Belden, when Paula wouldn't
stand up to Mr. Litchfield's verbal abuse, and most of
all when Paula told Sylvia she didn't see how she
could possibly leave the firm that had kept her
employed for years and promised a decent
retirement.

"All your life you've apologized, hidden, tried to
make yourself invisible, bent over backward not to

disturb or bother of annoy or in *any* way let other people know you exist, and you're doing it again!"

She had been right. Sylvia had almost always been right. And she had a deep, protective love for Paula. That gift was like armor. The armor Sylvia had worn for her at first, the battles she had fought in Paula's behalf, because of love. Stood up for her at the office and badgered Litchfield until Paula got her raise. And when Sylvia moved, Paula almost moved with her. Almost. But didn't. It wasn't done. How did you do it? Did you simply say, "I want this" and go after it? Just like that? The way all the young people seemed to be doing. Had she been wrong?

Wrong not in loving Sylvia but in her fear of pursuing it. The sadness touched her now gently, like a silk scarf against her neck. She moved her fingers to her throat. Let her fingertips caress her own coarsened skin.

She watched the silver, cool surface of the lake. It, too, was her armor. As if Sylvia, in leaving, had dropped the silver shield there, waiting for Paula to pick it up. It was time.

She needed nothing after all. She was not separate and unprotected. She felt something inside give way and let go, felt Sylvia's love flow into her and become her own. Sylvia's arms wrapped around her waist. She felt the absence now not absence at all but presence. Her own.

She could no longer be the woman she was, who had offered more than she could afford to give. Giving where she had not really wanted, denying herself the one person who never demanded anything, who had, in fact, given Paula everything. But that was all right now. Now she knew that Sylvia had always understood, had always forgiven her.

Many residents sent their letters to the alderman after Mrs. Shyamhari's accident. Three weeks later, walking home on a bright day with real spring in the air, Paula saw the new signs on Sheridan Road, eye level, announcing that violators—any cyclists over the age of twelve who rode on the sidewalks—would be arrested.

"This will show those hooligans," Dima announced triumphantly. Paula had not resisted when he offered to accompany her to the lake and back. Mrs. Goldstein said the signs were useless, that the police would never bother to catch cyclists until somebody got hurt. Paula wondered. Perhaps the police *would* get the hooligans. Eventually, people would pay attention, be more careful. Some of them, anyway.

"You know another storm could come and wash us all away before you get back," Dima said. "You might come back and have no building, no apartment."

She smiled. They turned at Granville, where she picked up her cleaning.

"Oh, I don't suppose everything will wash away. It's spring now, Dima. No more bad storms. And I'll bring you something nice to remind you of home."

"I already told you, I want nothing from that place."

"I know," she said, smiling warmly at him. "*Ya znayoo*," you silly but lovable *durak*."

He helped her carry the clothes in their plastic. They turned up Kenmore toward Rosemont. Suddenly, a bright patch of green burst into view. Someone had replaced the torn-up lawn at one of the cheaper apartment buildings. A small, decorative white fence surrounded the small yard with tiny

inverted hoops. A fresh bed of petunias nestled into
the yard next door. Purple and red and pink blooms.
A young, pretty black woman, wearing red cotton
slacks and a blouse with a stylish abstract design,
turned into the building's walkway.

"*Chornies*," Dima muttered. He saw none of the
colors, only the black skin.

Paula said nothing. She realized he saw as he saw.
He saw her as his. He saw black people as danger.
He saw the Soviet Union as his unforgivable enemy.
He saw the lake about to devour the shoreline as an
incontrovertible threat. As perhaps it was. All loss,
all change. Paula preferred, today, to see the bright
colors, the warm spring day: let's keep a lawn. Let's
look fine.

In the lobby Mrs. Shyamhari was walking without
crutches.

"Good as new," she told them. "And the new
signs warn everyone about riding on the sidewalk.
But I will always look carefully."

"Good," Dima said. "And if you see someone
riding, you call the police right away." Dima liked
the police. He needed the police to watch over all the
things that were after him, after the innocent,
hardworking people of the world. For him, the
American police and the American military were
angels more powerful even than the KGB devils.

Paula said goodbye to him at her apartment door,
and did not invite him in. In two days she would be
on the plane to Russia. She brewed a pot of tea and
took it to Sylvia's table at the window. She sat and
watched the lake. She touched her wrinkled cheeks,
the same cheeks Sylvia had once taken in her palms
and caressed with a kind of reverence. The light
came in the window and bathed her forehead in

gentle warmth. Her face was like the beach. Younger, she had used a rough sponge to abrade her skin, clear the dead cells away. Now her skin was going its own way, falling into ridges and dropping away from her bones as it pleased.

The condos were falling. Next year the waves could crash against the buildings again. Other tenants might move out again. So should she, perhaps. Yet she had no silk couches, no oriental rugs to be flooded. Just her old sofabed, her plain beige rug. Harder to pull herself up in the mornings, harder to pull the bed out.

She closed her eyes as she felt the warmth spreading softly across her face. It would be so tempting one day to fall asleep, let the waves roll over her, she a ripple in the beige rug turned to sand. She would lie flat and wait. The dream would come back. A dream of another sand. Years ago she had fallen from the sky into sand that parted to sift her through. Had honed her limbs, edged her heart, her hands into useful nets. Now she would catch nothing any longer, would cling to nothing, would let all the edges fade and blur.

Years ago she had clung to everything to fill her. But no more. She had what she came for. Now she needed nothing. No one to call, no one to see her, no one to notice or accuse, to run toward or away. She was becoming sand, her skin waiting for waves to come washing through the window. Waiting for no reason. When the waves came, she would rise, free and weightless, into the brightness of sky over the lake. Farther and farther. The clouds would take her up into their soft gray wool because they would have to, just as she would rise to meet them, moving because she had stopped trying not to.

Conversations with an Absent Lover on a Beachless Afternoon

1

I can assure you that the last thing I want to do is scare you off, away, further than you are going already to go because you are, in your own words, just starting your life, and I, by my own account, am half-way done. It is not my intention to stop you. No one stopped me, try as he—or she—might. I kept moving, like a shark, in one concentrated direction. No, never has anyone stopped me. Nor can anything, short of death.

2

When I was seven years old, my papi and the boys left on a two week vacation to Mexico. He didn't have a steady job. No matter. Mami did. She, being a good Mexican woman, did not try to stop him. She kept working, said nothing to the neighbors. I, taking her lead, did not utter a word of his absence to anyone either. Two weeks passed. The boys had rented a ten room villa in Cuernavaca. They were living the high life. Late night collect phone calls until my mother wouldn't accept anymore. She couldn't afford them, she told him. Six months passed. Papi showed up early one morning, just before Mami left for work. It was still dark. After the high life, the maid, the gardener and his family, the chauffeur, the parties with Hollywood Stars, Elizabeth Taylor (sans Eddie Fisher, or was it

Richard, by then?), the tailor made shark-skinned
suits, he came back without so much as the suitcase
he left with. Chuckie, the leader of the boys, stayed
behind to do five years in a Mexican prison, taking
the rap for the marijuana trafficking they had had
going—and that had kept them in that nouveau riche
lifestyle. Papi woke me up, who by then had become
Mami's bedmate and was in her/their bed lost in my
sleep. Papi. A big hug. He brought me a small sea
shell on a keychain, painted with a tiny palm tree
and on which was written, "Cuernavaca."

3

Before you came to my apartment some four, five
weeks ago, and it was all electricity and loneliness
and cigarettes and cheap wine, and did I also have
beer with you? You had come to talk to the writer
and ended with staying the weekend. When you left
on Sunday night, you preferred to walk back home,
left your motorcycle in the parking lot, needing to
leave some thing behind, proof that it had all really
happened.

4

Papi and the boys went out every Friday and
Saturday night. They liked to go to the jazz clubs, to
the Rego Theatre, to the Aragon Ballroom. They
heard Charlie "Bird" Parker, Stan Getz, Cal Tjader
on the xylophone, Willie Bobo, Mongo Santamaria.
They dressed in their best suits, rode up in Cadillacs,
gave big tips to the parking valets. Cadillac Ming
was the mechanic of the crowd and he kept all their
rides running like Rolls Royces. We lived on the
second floor in the back of a, not to be cliché but
truthful here, rat and roach infested flat. It was a

little scary coming home after dark because bums
and cutthroats hid under the stairs leading up to our
porch, shooting up, pissing, drinking whiskey.
After the show, the boys went down to Chinatown
to Lucky's, an all night Cantonese joint where Papi
always ordered the same thing: beef egg foo young.
When I moved to California, moons and decades
later, he said there were no good Chinese restaurants
there, because none served egg foo young, or at least
not like what he had been used to at Lucky's. Mami
liked Chinese food, too. So, at about two or three in
the morning, when Papi got home, he'd wake her up.
With him, he'd have those little white boxes, packed
with cold hard white rice and in another, Chinese
greens, because greens were Mami's favorite. She was
never the prissy type about food. She could eat
anything, at least once, just to try. She ate frog legs
once. When she watched a t.v. show, and there was a
dinner scene, Mami lost interest in the dialogue and
tried her best to figure out what it was they were
eating, wanting to taste it.

5

"Here's the thing," I start to say to you, this
morning. My head is pounding and you have been
talking about taking off, leaving to start your life, to
end your days as a student and become a (a frightful
thought you) responsible member of society, of your
family, be a good son, going back home right after I
return from New York, leaving with no promises. I
am not a college sophomore. It means nothing to me
if you can make no promises. I am worried about
today. The work I have to do, the writing I must slit
wrists to get to, my own slick, ceaseless motion going
linearly forward into the vast open terrain of

nothingness. "What's the thing?" You jab at me. I can see it is true what all the faculty on campus fear about partying, even once, with students. They lose all respect for you. Once they've caught you with your pants down, so to speak, there's no getting a break. "See? You don't even know what the thing is." You tease and I am still groping for the thing, the thing that I know. Only how do I tell it to you?

6

His birthday is tomorrow, but twenty two years ago, on that day, Mami busted him with his girlfriend. A beautiful Polish girl who was twenty-four at the time. Papi was thirty-five. Mami had bought him a couple of cool sports shirts as a present. She also bought him a new set of timbales. Because our landlord did not let us play music in the flat, he said he had taken them over to Chuckie's house. Papi had been out all night, got home that morning, pretty loaded, said he had been thrown in the drunk tank. Mami had taken to searching his pockets by then, and found a cleaners ticket. There was our last name on it but with an address that was not our address.

Even though we left Papi sleeping, by the time we got to that address—which was far away, in the white section of town—his Cadi was parked right in front. Mami pushed upon the door. There he was, dressed in one of the new birthday sports shirts. It had black and white stripes, kind of like the pattern that umpires wear, I think, or at least, that's what it reminded me of, and as always, he was wearing his shades.

Annette, because she had a name now, it was Annette, and very suitable too, was petite and had her hair frosted. She was sitting on the couch across from Papi, who sat, cross-legged on a lazy boy chair, in a way that made you think it was his chair, his place in that room. They had not so much as stirred when Mami and I burst in. Obviously, they were waiting for us. They had had a big row the night before, Annette began to babble. She was trying to break up with him because he would not leave his wife. He forced his way into her house. His arms were covered with fingernail scratches. She had called the cops. Mami was never any good with English, but she did a good job getting her point across then and there. "So here are the timbales I bought you for your birthday!" And pas! The timbales went flying in a loud way, and the albums, too, that Mami knew were his, Perez Prado, Machito, Ray Barretto, his man.

"Just tell me one thing, Mingo," Annette said, from the frozen place on her couch, "Do you love me?" Mami stops flailing things about and looks at him. I am looking at him, too. He is just too cool behind those dark glasses. Then, expressionless, he says, "Yeah, I love you, Annette."

7

"Is it true the you wouldn't show up to speak at our class because the professor wouldn't pay you?" You asked me last night when you came. "You wouldn't lie to me, would you? Otherwise nothing we have said to each other means anything. The thing is, I mean, the professor said that about you, but I knew better. I knew he was lying, lying to boost himself up, to make us think you are that way. I know that the truth is, he can't stand the fact that you are in demand and that he's not anymore. And

the sad part of it is, *I* have read his stuff, and the
man used to be bad (bad meaning real good here)
and it's just too bad he has to act that way now
toward younger writers coming up. But have some
pity on him. One day, a younger writer is going to
come up behind you and you will know how that
feels..."

"*That* will never happen," I tell you. I am, after
all, a writer, not a dancer. If I know anything, am
sure of one blessed fact about this life that I have
been leading, it is that. *I* will never depend on my
past glories because *my* work just gets better. I get
better, and I am going to keep it up until I drop dead
with a pen in my hand."

8

"He was very proud of you," Ash Can told me at
the wake. Ash Can, who more than Papi, could never
hold down a job. Mexico, dope, music, women, all
the same stuff. "And I, of him," I answered.

9

I have this friend who is a writer. She says her
lovers hate the fact that she fictionalizes everything
that happens between them. Even in the throes of a
heated argument, she will have to stop to take notes,
telling herself, remember how he looked when he
said this, remember what you were wearing, and
exactly how it felt to say such and such. And they
hate it, her lovers. She writes pretty tight stories, too.
She doesn't give a hill of beans what they feel about
it. There are always more lovers. There are always
more stories to write.

Papi did not like the book I wrote for him. I knew
this because he said nothing about it. But when he

came to see me, after a few beers, I knew he would say something and he did. "I feel like my life is an open book," he said. (Just like Mingo to come up with that.) But I was all too ready with my reply, since the family moratorium on my book. "It isn't your life," I said. "It is my life. And it isn't your book. It's mine."

10

"So, you are going off to live your life, that's okay," I tell you this morning. "You will go back home, you will travel, you will get a job and pay back your school loans..."

"Hey! This is *my* life we're talking about," you say, resenting the underlying lack of enthusiasm, my obvious bad attitude. "You say I am going to travel in the same tone of voice as paying back my loans. Traveling is *supposed* to be exciting."

"Yes, you will have a good time. You will have your adventures in Mexico, you will meet your pseudo innocent twenty year olds, you will sit in an open air cafe and drink beer with your brother and you will say to yourself, '*She* is somewhere right this minute, sitting in an open air cafe getting drunk.' And what you are doing at that moment will feel no different than working and paying off your loans because *I* won't be with you and you'll be wondering where I am..."

"And with *who*," you add, not looking at me, the way you usually say things to me when you just can't say them to my face, into these eyes embedded with just too many memories for any given lifetime.

11

One night my parents were in a hotel in
Cuernavaca. I had left home long before that, but
had decided to catch up with them on their vacation
at the border. It was about two a.m. and I was
coming back from Mexico City with my aunt. She is
pretty lively, so we both had the same idea about
bringing back some musicians from the zocalo to the
hotel to serenade my parents. "What is this?" My
father asked, sticking his messed up hair, sleepy head
outside their room. The three musicians playing, "Mi
Viejo San Juan," and my tía and I serving up mescal
to everyone.

Because my tía has had a life of being
misunderstood, her joie de vivre, her laughter, her
parties, despite five children and forty years in a
seamstress sweatshop, she decided that night that I
should have been *her* daughter instead of the one she
has that now has seven children of her own. But me,
she said, I am like her, *I* know how to live.

12

"There's something to be said about innocence,"
you said to me last weekend, when I snatched you
away on a rendezvous, to meet my friends, to see
theatre, Almodovar's latest film, to drink at a Latino
transvestite bar. You said this with regards to the
twenty year old you had decided (not without some
reservation) to send on her way so that you could
spend more time with me, and had struggled with
how to tell her because you so much did not want to
hurt her feelings. Innocence was something that she
could give you and I could not, you said. Innocence
in females to feed the male ego had its place in
nineteenth century novels. Also, always in Mexican

society. Was it a given that all my male lovers be older, better educated, more savvy about the ways of the world, so that I, in my supposedly natural terrain as the perennial apprentice, would serve as the static symbol of the innocence with they so much yearned to believe exists in this havoc called a world that they themselves have invented? Once innocence—an all too brief state of being, if such a one exists at all—encounters experience it is transformed; and if it is understood, it becomes knowledge, and if it is employed, then that is wisdom. I so much prefer the wisdom in your eyes to the innocence of your remarks.

13

Was Papi looking for innocence in Annette? There was the same age difference between her and him as you and me. The facialist looked at me, and being Californian, she read my "aura" before applying herbal clay masks and steam. "At first, I thought that your eyes held lots and lots of sadness," she said. Yes, I have contained death in each of these eyes like two dams, holding it all back, holding in its definitiveness during these prolonged months in this tiny city by the sea, which is beautiful, yet not my home. I have no home now, so I wait to leave. "But no," she thinks, after an hour of talking and doing things to bring color back to my skin. I am not pale, by any means. I am dark like the Earth (and you are too, more so, mi amor). But I have gone yellow, sallow, I think they call it. "No," she says, reflectively, "Those are survivor eyes. You are a poet. There is wisdom, much, much wisdom you have brought to us here to help heal this planet. Be good to yourself. Find someone who will make you laugh."

You only need to laugh to bring back that glow you radiate from your inner being. Poets are doing very important work. But they must protect themselves because they feel everything."

14

"You are so wise, m'amor," I say to you last night, when you have shown so much compassion for the professor who chose to tell the class that all I am concerned about these days is making money. You think I am making fun of you. Who has ever called you wise? My child is not yet seven, and I learn from him every day, how to see things, how to keep opening myself to giving when I am certain that one more layer ripped away from my being will cause me to die from overexposure and yet, no, I do not, I continue, and the more I give, the more the current of spiritual generosity becomes circular and profuse. You are wise and you make me laugh and I am sure you have come to my life, not out of innocence. Neither you nor I were ever innocent. It is just that way with some people. "You will have to record my memoirs," I tell you. "Maybe that's what I am destined to do," you wonder. No, you are destined to live your very own life, and among the things you might choose to do along the way, is to remember me. You don't have to write it down. Just remember me.

15

"So the thing is this," I say, after you have some coffee, and I know that I can feel that dragon called what I do breathing fire inside me. "I am not polished, I am not whip cream, I have to do it raw. All the voices of those who call writing a craft, who speak grammatically correct, who have studied with this name or that, well up in my head and tell me once again, I have no business doing what I am doing. I don't have enough credits, no validating Guggenheim, no South of France-New York poet in residency, nada, hombre, just me, escaping and moving and trying not to remember, but writing it down anyway. Too many have called me a tonta, a dummy, a brown spic india from the streets and left me there. Papi only wanted five grandchildren from me. Dummy, he called me, after I graduated with an M.A. from the Ivy League. "What you need is a novio," my mother told me the other day over the phone—afraid that maybe my only having women friends meant I had gone the other way, and who will there be to protect me, she worries, to validate my existence, "Get yourself a dishwasher...don't aim so high!"

16

"Tell me a fantasy," I ask. We're in a dive in San Francisco. I am drinking margaritas out of a water glass. It is late afternoon. We will be leaving shortly, and the rendezvous will be over.

"We will have a church wedding, mariachis y todo."

"Will your family be there?"

"Of course!"

"And will your mother give the groom away to the bride?"

"Of course! And we'll even slaughter a pig!"

17

In another life, I was pregnant in Puerto Rico and didn't know it. I only knew that every day that we

were there I was nauseous and couldn't stay awake.
One Saturday, the men brought a big, fat pig up to
the house. Papi held it down while they slit its throat
over a huge tub. On Sunday, we went to the country
and had lechón. Well, at least the rest did. I slept. I
was sick. I was pregnant and didn't know it. Months
before, having lost all pretenses of innocence, the
"father" had begun to be cruel to me, despising the
fact that I had dared to love him as an equal.

18

Enough is enough. "Tell me to stop loving you," I
say. It isn't any fun anymore when the thought of
coming apart from you will leave splinters in my
side, in my lips, my nipples, the soles of my feet.
"Tell me, 'Apolinar, don't count on me.'" I put it
another way, "Tell me to blow you off."

"Why would I want to say a silly thing like that?"
is all you answer whenever I say that.

19

Mami decided the best thing was a divorce. Over
fifteen years of womanizing and loneliness and her
working the assembly line and the final straw was
the day a new woman she was training at work told
her she knew Papi. She had worked with him at the
plant where he was at at the time. "No, it's
impossible!" She told Mami, "Domingo Espinoza
can't be your husband!" "but it's true!" Mami
said—innocently. "Here is a picture of him. Here is a
picture of our children...we've been married for
nearly sixteen years!" "No, it's impossible!" The
woman insisted incredulously. "Domingo Espinoza is
not married. He lives with his mother. She's old and
that's why no one can ever go to their house. But he

is *living* with this Polish girl. They plan to get married. Moreover, there was this other woman, a Puerto Rican girl, at the plant. She even showed off an engagement ring he had given her! What a ruckus she raised at the factory the day she found out about the *güera!*"

20

I've seen Mami drunk, smashed, completely loaded, bombed, twice in my life. The first time was at the end of that day. When I got home from work, she had a half empty bottle of Cutty Sark in her hand. Papi's shirts were all laid out on the bed. Whenever he got home, she was going to send him packing to the Polish girl. The other time was the night before I left for Europe to do research on a new novel. I was leaving my fifteen month old infant in the care of his father, in her care, in the care of my family and with a good family friend, who also cared. To her mind, I was abandoning my baby. Bad mother, I am. Bad mother, bad wife. No good woman.

That evening, over two decades ago, when Papi got home, he told Mami she was silly for listening to gossips. He put all his shirts back into the closet and sat down at the table for her to serve him his supper.

21

Mami has given me a lot of bad advice. One of the things was that no matter what was going on between my man and me, I should always have food prepared for him to eat, whenever he got home. When I got wind that this was particularly bad advice, as innocent as it may appear, or at least, as harmless, was just last summer. I was waiting for my

son's father to get back to his house with our child.
We had been split up for some time, but I don't
know, it was nostalgia perhaps, most likely it was
Mami's bad advice that caused me to decide to cook.
How nice for him to find a warm meal waiting. I
baked a chicken, prepared a salad. After a while they
got home, the child, his father, and the current
woman in his life. "Here," he said to her, "Sit down.
Have something to eat."

Oh, but I should have learned that lesson some
time before. It was, after all, the reason why I left to
begin with. A young woman from out of town. He
was just being courteous, he said, showing her
around. I made chicken then, too. One of his favorite
things, you know. She came over. He said to her,
"Here, sit down. Have something to eat." The next
night, he went out. She too, was gone. They were
both away all night. The following morning, I too,
was gone.

22

At this point, you will want to take all this, I'm
sure, and neatly Freudianalyze me to explain why I
have preferred women's companionship over men's
lately. Did you simply tolerate my feminist seminar?
Didn't you hear my whole rap about the history of
patriarchy, the repression of female sexuality,
institutionalization of religion, etc.? I haven't felt at
liberty to discuss with you the dynamics of the
intimacies between women. Women are no angels.
Oh, we are no innocents, not for a moment. What
we do when we are alone behind closed doors and
the things we say to each other and the horrendous
violence that we bring from the world to each other
and make our own, because all of us know that Eve

was no betrayer. She was a sage holding on to humanity, to save us all. But for the time being, she's been beaten.

23

"I am so proud of you," Papi said on his death bed, a few days before he left us, holding my new novel in his hand, impressive for its weight. Even writers are impressed with it, unread, because of its size. "And I, of you," I said, holding the draft of my new manuscript in my hand. He was dying and I was writing. Trying to figure it out. The thing. The thing of it is. The guys who came to replace his oxygen supply were impressed. "You wrote all these books?" they said, smiling, kind of nervous and flustered in the presence of someone with so much discipline. "Yeah," I head one whisper to the other, "And so beautiful, too."

When they left, Papi's eyes were bright. "Did you see how impressed those guys were with your books?" I nodded. "I'm going to read this," he said, "As soon as I'm feeling a little better. Once I can get up and around again." Papi. He was going to read something I had written. Everybody was impressed. A big fat book with a glossy cover and my simple picture with the direct gaze on the back. Papi. Read what I wrote? Oh my god. He, who had never thought of this being that had sprung from the womb of a woman who served him for forty years and now, what would he think of the monster I had become? The thoughts I have. The godless, female thoughts, I have. And speak. And write. And what's more—people out there, important people with the power and command to publish are putting them out for the whole world to see. To him, their opinion of it all meant it must be worth reading, after all.

24

"I hope I never get that disciplined about anything," you say.

"And that's why you show so much potential, I respond. Go on. Go away. Leave this place. I am leaving it, too. We have both paid our dues here. Take your thrift shop Remington to an island and type standing up as Hemingway did, or kneeling over the toilet in a cheap hotel, like Kerouac. You have your heroes ready made. "What will you think of me the next time you see me?" You asked this morning. This morning when we teeter-tottered between forever-and-never-again-and-must-we-decide-now-and-if-only-I-could-just-walk-away-how-much-easier -that-would-make-things for us, for you, but mostly for me. I have a birthday coming up soon. I am pre-menopausal. I have earned it all, so it's okay to say it, even to you, especially to you. "It all depends on what we say to each other when we part," I say, accepting that we are going to part soon, and more than this, not wanting to be with anyone who would want to part from me.

25

A few days after I left him, I got a call. Papi had called in a priest. I caught a plane within the hour and by that afternoon, I was with him at the hospital. "Don't let him see you cry," my sister told me just before I walked into his room. "se nos va, hija," Mami said, once I could let go of his hand, take my lips from his sweaty forehead. He is leaving us. "Papi, we have been so lucky knowing you," I

whispered. Many interminable hours passed. I drove
the rest of the family out, making too much noise,
putting out too much weird energy, as they say in
California. "What do you want, Papi?" I whispered.
We were alone. He was all mine. My charming,
handsome, young father with the pianist's hands, too
poor to learn to play the instrument of his choice, so
when he did a short stint in a suitcase factory thirty
years ago, he learned to sound out tones from the
various suitcases and became a percussionist instead.
I have his delicate thin-finger hands. I also did not
get piano lessons, though I would have preferred to
do anything, but this that I do, which is soundless
and so without rhythm. "Do you want me to pray
for you?" I whispered. He shook his head, gasping
heavily for his last breaths. "Get me...something...for
the pain." I did. Papi died in his sleep.

26

"I love, love to sleep with you," I have whispered
to you some mornings when the sheets cling to us,
and there's no point in getting up because all we can
do is sleep, sleep together. "Why?" you ask me.
Because it is like being born, the first moments, the
blindness, the dark, the departure from the
moistness. My twin embryo. Your body is like mine
only more angular, limbs entwined like gnarled
branches. You snore a little. I get up a dozen times. I
always come back. Hold you. I cannot explain
anything about this, about why you nearly cried
feeling the pain of a writer, a woman you didn't
know, why I invited you to my home, why it feels
like something is fractured, an ankle bone, a wrist,
when you go away, why I always know you'll come
back, scratching like a tomcat at my back door. I

only know sleeping eases the pain and then, the pain itself is not so horrible but becomes a crystal of sharp, translucent points, through which I perceive all that cannot be put into words.

27

"What will make you happy?" I asked that first weekend when you came and did not leave. "Truthfully?" you asked, "a poem."

I was so smitten with my new lover, who made me laugh, who reminded me so of Domingo when he was a very young man and could not stop to think of a wife and children and a baby daughter who had nothing to do with him except for having the same hands and feet, that I set upon the task of fulfilling that request.

And once I gave you the poem, handwritten on a postcard of two lovers kissing, you showed it around. "Leave those women be!" One friend ribbed you and you said, not as long as you were serving as such inspiration.

"Here are two more," I said, then, poems on cards, a woman breastfeeding, another of a street photographer in Guatemala, a sign over his head that read "Recuerdo." "And when you show them to your friend, tell him this:

'If she were a seamstress, she would have made me a shirt of pure silk, white as an angel's dream, with mother of pearl buttons; each eyelet hand embroidered with silver thread—that I might wear around town, and the women think me handsome and the men, think me rich.

'If she were a shoemaker, she would have made me boots, custom fitted, patent leather and burgundy colored, up to the knee, like those worn by the gauchos in Patagonia.

'If she were a cook, she would have prepared a feast like those that were served the emperor daily before the fall of the Empire, a feast of turkey and mole, quail, and chocolate, enough to feed all those in that palace—but forbidding anyone to touch a morsel for himself, until I was done, washed, and fast into my siesta.

'But no, this one only writes verses. They are useless to anyone. They can't keep you warm, satisfy your stomach's yearning. You cannot gamble with them when you have lost your money, your shoes, and your coat. Who would give a dime for a poem? no, she is only a poet of sorts. Moreover, they come easy to her. Women, after all, are all romantics.'"

28

"You have a daughter who has published a book and yet, she got you working here," Papi told me a woman who also worked the graveyard shift at the factory said to him when he showed her my first book of poems. Papi said he had only shrugged his shoulders. If I made money from my poems, he thought, it was my money, not his.

In the factory, people equated books with money and money with freedom from the drill press, from losing fingers, and from lazy foremen who tallied up your rates, threatening always that without your quota tomorrow you would be bumped and out of a job altogether. Never mind that they were poems, virtually worthless on the domestic market. It was a book and people who wrote books were important and important people had money.

Rare is the one who can love a poem, who will wear it like a new hat, who will lick it clean like an ice-cream cone, who will cry over it, talk with it, tell it all his secrets—share it with a friend. Rare, are you.

29

You, at twenty three, loverboy, have never been left, you say. Your family members, mother, father, each one intact. Except through death, I too, have not been left. We announce this to each other, like two opponents in the ring, as if to leave were a victory of some sort, even through death. Would it not be better to say, I stayed. I simply loved and I did not want to leave. Leaving is for the defeatist, the egotist, the one who is not worthy of the love he is choosing to dismiss.

Perhaps not.

Except through death, I don't know what parting is. And you, in that dramatic manner of some when they are young, are certain you are not destined here for long—all because you have enjoyed life too much, lavished yourself with its sweet aroma, shamelessly adored it. We are told that to love the world is to earn condemnation. I, too, thought I would die young. I dreamt it. I told my father to comfort him, it will be me, first of all, to leave the rest. I even tried to provoke it with pills. I had remembered that once, when he was the age I am now, after too many beers, had slumped in a chair and began to weep, "I don't want to die. I am afraid of dying..."

But it was he, not me, who left first, and without pretense, quite unwillingly. I think he would have preferred to see anyone die before himself, he loved his life so—just breathing; attached to the things in his surroundings, the VCR, new CD player, the neighbors he got on well with and even those with whom he didn't and those surviving old friends. His desire to stay had nothing to do with me. He did not even say goodbye, though I had been with him, holding his hand, wiping his brow, keeping the oxygen mask in place, ceaselessly for six hours. Instead, he asked me to open the hermetically sealed hospital windows, to open wide the door. Air. All he wanted and needed on that winter night was air.

30

"You are earth and air and sky to me," I wrote in my verse to you. And I, in turn, have become what? Rock and stone, sediment and ash. The poet who was never a poet but a sharp shooting female who blew men off like cans off a tree stump, came home to bury her father. She took the money she had earned from the poems that were for him, and bought his coffin. She learned about the added requirement of a vault and paid for that. She went with her mother and sister and picked out two plots, one for the mother, next to the father's, located next to a large statue of St. Peter.

"When I die, Silvia," she asked her sister, suddenly all too aware that no matter how far she traveled away from these people bound to her by blood, they would own her, even after death, "just cremate me, okay? Don't fuss over me. Don't go to any expense. It's not worth it." Her elder sister, the good Catholic, stared, horrified at the extent of her sister's sacrilege. "Get away from me," she told her, "You are going to burn in hell and take me with you."

"No, Silvia," the poet protested—as poets are wont to do—"You don't understand. You will only go to hell if you believe in hell."

"Well, I do."

"Well, then, *you're* in big trouble."

31

Your mother was locked up in her room on her wedding night by her husband while he went out carousing, you said, weeping. Imagine that life! You cried. A good Mexican son crying over his sacred, suffering mother's life, bearing too many children, fallen womb, cancer of the uterus from birth control, and the husband who never had thought her good enough for him.

My sister was beaten on the street on her wedding night by her groom, twenty five years ago, I could have told you. His whole family looked on. I alone jumped on top of him, pounded on him, forced him to stop.

My cousin has had seven children. She is not allowed to have visitors. She does not have a telephone. Her husband has kept her imprisoned for nearly twenty years.

But you did not want to hear about other women. Your mother is the only woman that matters. The things I will never write about, I sum up and say, "I once led the life of a dog." You say nothing.

32

The sun has begun to set. I cannot see them from here, from these dark rooms that I have inhabited for the past ten months, more transient than tourist my life has become, but I know voluminous clouds are hovering over the mountain peaks. There will be no fog tonight. I have opened up the wine. I've gone back to smoking cigarettes. I think that some time tonight you'll come back, not because you want to, would not prefer the company of friends, those who have been with you these recent years, fellow students, preparing for your lives, when everything is left to the expanse and promise of the future; and not because you don't detest obligation, nor that you are not susceptible to committing acts you dislike out of guilt. But because...we believe (and I too, have said as much here), that we move straight, that we travel forward, but we don't. We move in spirals. When there seems to be only future, the spirals are so wide, for a time we believe ourselves to be moving in a straight line. But after a while, we begin to feel familiar with what appears to be new, and that is because the spirals are becoming tighter, and finally, small ringlets.

That is why you will come back—a man in a ringlet of fire.

33

Every night, without fail, after his death I dreamt of him. I dreamt him as an aberration. I knew he was dead but I would have him back any way I could. Sometimes I dreamt myself without feet, learning to walk on crutches, to adapt myself to this reality without him. One night or morning, the dreams stopped. Then one night, not long after, you came to this place where I live. You looked around, and out of vanity, or desire, or simply needing a place to stay, you announced, "This feels like home. You should let me come live with you."

34

It was a long time since I talked to a man, in the twilight, in shadows, kissed his hands, heard his secrets, told him my own. Don't turn on the light, you warn me, when you are crying. Otherwise, you become bullyish, resentful of me if I catch a glimpse of your tears. That night of his birthday, so many years ago, after he left Annette's apartment on his own and met us at his brother's house, where we were having a party in his honor, he began to cry. I don't know why he cried. I don't know why you cry. "Comfort your father," my mother told me. "You are so cold. She has always been so cold," she told the guests about me, as if I wasn't there. "Put your arms around him." She insisted, "Tell him to come home..."

35

Sometimes, I forget the limitations of this existence and think he is still planning on taking a plane, coming to see me this summer. Sometimes, I yearn for his voice on the phone, that easy manner of his, the vacant, repeated promise of "If there's anything you need, I'm here." I asked you this morning, "and when I go through this tunnel, this thing so popularly known these days as the writing process, when I write what I must write, not what I want to, not what anyone will want to read, just what I need to write, tell me you'll be at the other end. Say to me, 'Apolinar, let's go for a walk on the beach' or, 'Come, it's time to eat.' Remind me that I am still part of this world." If there's anything you need, I'm here. Instead, you kissed me, just as you always do before leaving. I tasted on your lips, your tongue, the

utter isolation of each man and woman and knew
you could not come back, then, no matter what.

Thanksgiving Day in Homicide

I've left the windows open on the unmarked car so I can hear the radio. It's Thanksgiving day, a slow day, and the park is deserted. A light snow is falling, and two clean black lines curve across the park to the back of the squad car, stopped abruptly against the expanse of white.

When the call comes in I'm looking closely at the red viburnum berries in the hedge—this variety is called high-bushcranberry—knobby clusters extending from skinny stems like tiny multiple fingers. I wish I had my camera; the light is soft, and the berries, some bright red droplets, others withering and brown, stand out against the fresh snow. I think how few people know of the variety of wildlife here, small animals and birds, in this park on the lakefront. There is so much winter food—crab apples as well as viburnum, and dogwood, and elderberry, and buckthorn.

"Homicide car 7704," the dispatcher calls again, and I sink a little as I answer; it's nearly time to go home, to join my family for Thanksgiving dinner. The call is a homicide in an apartment building on east 45th St. I write the time and location on my clipboard.

The snow has turned to gray slush in the streets. In front of the building a marked car and a paddy wagon are double-parked; as I approach along the sidewalk two uniformed officers are maneuvering a heavy stretcher down the front steps, the body covered in a bloody white sheet. I go in through the broken front door, past the torn mailboxes, up the cold stairway to a third floor apartment.

The room is hot and smells of cooking food. A boyish blonde patrolman is waiting. "You're not gonna believe this one," he says. He's grinning. His bravado annoys me.

"I'll believe it," I say, not smiling. Four years in homicide, he thinks he's going to tell me something new—he's going to tell me the unique, the strange, the funny, the ironic reason for this death; he's too dense to know that the reason is never the reason, that there isn't any reason, that if reason had any grip on the world, he and I would have to find another kind of work.

An old black woman sits in a straight-backed chair and stares at me, a reminder of Dachau. Gaunt, with spindly arms, the skin of her face stretched hard against her cheekbones, stretched around eye sockets so dark you can barely see the small eyes within; when I look at her she smiles, the mouth a toothless cavern.

There are jagged holes in the green walls, ribs of lathe exposed. The floor is bare and grimy black, with a large, bright red pool of blood in the middle of the room. A gas range sits in a doorless closet, all burners glowing blue under pots. By the smell, a turkey is roasting in the oven. The patrolman shows me the murder weapon, a butcher knife; he has wrapped the wooden handle in a bloody rag. The streaks of blood along the blade are already dried and brown. I want to tell him this isn't the way to handle evidence, but I don't.

He tells me what happened. The apartment has four rooms, a different family living in each. There is no kitchen—all share the common stove. A man accused another tenant of taking some of the beans he had been cooking on the stove; the accused man called him a liar and pushed him, and the cooker of beans took the butcher knife from the top of the stove and shoved the blade deep up under the other man's ribs.

I take statements from everyone except the old woman—she has told the patrolman she saw nothing. I am uneasy with her staring; each time I glance her way she smiles, opening the dark, oval hole of her mouth. I hurry to finish; leaving, I take the knife from the patrolman. As I go to the door she pursues me, and I realize now that I am afraid of her. She reaches out to me; the little shrivelled bulbs at the tips of her skinny fingers tug at my sleeve as she speaks in a hoarse whisper. I want to get away, but I bend down close to listen, my ear close to her mouth. Her breath smells like carrion.

"Please don't take my knife," she says. "I have nothing to carve the turkey."

Baby

Val double-parked in front of Passavant Hospital, making sure he didn't block the circular drive for ambulances and police cars. Lottie Mae wasn't waiting on the pavement like she said. It offered a way for him to dig at her when she got into the car, but he buried the impulse. He bit his nails and thought over the ways he could make it appear that her lateness was not an issue.

Strong-legged white women in nursing uniforms bustled through the revolving doors, adjusting bags, throwing sunglasses up to their eyes, disappearing into the heat and change-of-shift. He'd been parked there three minutes or so, enough time to catch the attention of a territorial meter maid ripping a ticket from her book and slapping it under a windshield wiper of an Austin-Healy a few cars down. Wilting passengers clumped up around the door of an exhaust-shrouded bus, patiently waiting as an old woman, refusing help, probed her way down the steps with a rubber-tipped cane.

He saw her come into the foyer through the sun-distorted plate glass. He started the engine. The meter maid walked by impassively, turning the pages of her ticket book in a casually threatening way.

He still couldn't get over the blond hair. His wife—a black woman with blond hair! In their senior year of high school she'd declared that black women who bleached their hair blond wanted to be white. Blond—he could not understand! She came out, pushing the revolving door, her lab coat draped

over her arm. He didn't like the coat. He had nothing
of comparable value in his life. Her reverence for it
angered him; she knew it. She opened the passenger
door, touched the seats, drew back frowning,
squinting into the glare and dusty traffic. He
stretched back and took a rough towel from the back
seat and tossed it to her. She covered the seat and got
in.

"Babyjack at home?" she asked.

"He wasn't there when I left. He might be there
now."

She exhaled and threw the lab coat between them.
He pulled away from the curb, and headed east
towards Lake Shore Drive, wondering how many
men she'd slept with during their separation.

If he didn't look at her for a while, anger might
not flare. If he looked straight ahead, put what
powers he had into driving, appearing worthwhile in
the eyes of blurred motorists and passersby, he'd
side-step her measuring, exacting existence, and get
beyond the impulse to say something cruel.

He had not spent the money she'd tossed to him
this morning to buy cigarettes. "Like I'm some kinda
dog," he'd thought for much of the day. He kept it in
his shirt pocket all day long to remind him of some
opaque feeling of hurting her by letting it rot in his
shirt pocket.

"You get out to Hotpoint today?" She asked.

"They ain't hiring," he responded.

"Did you put in an application?"

The hate and rage roiled and churned in him. He
felt constricted, as powerless as the cerulean oil and
water oceans trapped inside plexiglass cases. She
looked away, closing her eyes, leaning her head
against the headrest. She liked the sounds of

mufflers. He always had cars with strong, nice
sounding mufflers.

"Did you see Mrs. Penn today? You was s'posed
to pick up his report card today." She leaned
forward, bracing against the dashboard. "His
teacher, Val!"

"I know Mrs. Penn, Lottie Mae," he snapped,
pausing to make sure she knew her continuing doubt
was unnecessary. "He wasn't in school today," Val
explained. "I guess he didn't want to see the rest of
his class graduate without him. She wants to see both
of us. The principal and Mrs. McConkle, the social
worker, wants to see us tomorrow. They ain't gon' let
him back in school in the fall."

He could not think about it all. The thought of
Babyjack not going to high school, left behind,
saddened him. He wanted to escape the burden of
grief, stop the car, get out, leave again. Babyjack was
just an echo of the sweet thing he used to be. Val
opened himself to the blame, allowed himself to be
buffeted. He heard his son's voice submerged in the
marbleized anger swirling around them.

Once Lottie Mae told him of a recurring urge to
get out with the people walking by the lake, and put
her feet into the cold, blue-green water, to show all
of the half-naked white folks how open and friendly
she could be. She told him she wanted to buy her
first bathing suit and sit in the sand watching the
long shadows from tall buildings across Lake Shore
Drive creep out over the water. He'd never taken
them to the beach. He knew she wanted him to do
some of the family things white men did with their
children. He thought about the ease and
mindlessness with which white people oiled and
displayed their bodies. He wondered what

weightiness, if any, accompanied their ability to take off their clothes in public. The image of Lottie Mae in her bathing suit faded as they drove through the park.

At the top of the steps she turned and looked down at him. As he stood looking up at her from the second floor landing, he thought that his footfalls had annoyed her.

"You think you need to go out lookin' for him?" she said.

"Say it like you thinkin' it Lottie Mae! You mean you want me to go out lookin' for him."

She put her balled fist on her hip.

"Why should I have to say anything? Don't you want to go lookin' for him? He yo' child too." Stung again. He could not answer her. She paid no attention to him as he tried to invent terror between the narrow slits of his eyes.

Larry, the landlord, had kept his promise. The smell of the newly painted back porches filled the hallway.

"Let me git a glass-a-water and take a piss," he said, knowing she hated how leisurely he moved towards what had to be done. She unlocked the door. Cool, pine scented air rushed from the darkened apartment as the sounds of the tumbler echoed in the hallway. He'd mopped the floors. He sensed that his attempts at trying to smooth over a year and a half of separation angered her. He wished he'd left the floors dirty.

"You know he ain't s'pose to be hangin' with Hung Young no mo'." She removed her shoes and went into the kitchen for a cup of ice cubes. The half-built model of a gas driven P38 Lightning sparkled under the lamp in Babyjack's room. She switched off his lamp and pulled his door shut.

"The longer he stay runnin' wit 'im, the further he gittin' away from us." He stood away from her as she ripped the ice cubes from the metal tray and threw them into a clear water glass. He felt that what went on inside of the hospital made her able to get right to bone. He feared and wanted that in her.

He knew now that whatever made her want him so badly at one time, no longer existed. He felt on his own now. The swift and bloodless manner with which she responded to him frightened him into knowing she no longer wanted to be responsible for him.

As he went out he heard a strong, male voice, maybe Brook Benton, singing "Walk on the Wildside" float up from the McFadden's second floor landing. He passed their door. Laughter and talk, the smell of boiling greens and pork streamed innocently, without distress, from behind their door.

Back in the car, he drove down North Park, towards the school yard. Clusters of school kids straggled and cavorted down the street, their graduation ribbons fluttering from stiff new suits and dresses, on their way to Latisha's party. Aimlessly, the names of Sharinda, Shamika, Calvin, Booker T., Latonya, Danika, and Ahmahl whooped through the stinging afternoon heat. From these disembodied voices Val wished that he'd heard his son's name.

"MIKO DEAD," newly spray painted, shouted from the chaos of semi-realized epithets scrawled on the green metal doors of the school. School let out hours ago. Babyjack was not on the basketball court. Maybe he went to Lincoln Park since school was out for the summer now, maybe to the big lagoon or the boathouse at North Avenue Beach. Maybe he went to the projects. Hung Young lived in 1117.

He went up Wells street to Division and down Larrabee into Cabrini. He drove slowly past the three main buildings, hoping that he'd see him among the people moving about out front. The buildings reminded him of stacked bird cages. Heat waves snaked up from the pavement as a sweating couple, each carrying brown paper shopping bags, disappeared into the soft, cavernous shadows near the elevators.

He didn't want to search for him. The guilt associated with this reality settled into a repository where he shelved everything he could not act upon. Babyjack's indifference cut deeper than Lottie's disinterest. When he considered what both of them thought of him, he flinched, and squeezed the padded steering wheel. The first night he moved back in Lottie made him sleep in the basement on the super's spare cot near the furnace. She had to think it over. He had covered himself with *Chicago American* newspapers stacked along the wall. That night, amid the trace smells of bituminous coal and something decomposing, he imagined or dreamed himself in hell. Just before going to sleep, he relived childhood fears of werewolves, vampires, being alone on a southern road in the dead of night.

The next morning, she stood watching him sleep for a time before waking him. When he awoke he realized the brightness filling the basement came from her radiant white lab uniform. The gold hoops on her ears and her bright yellow hair, drawn stiff and immovable around her oval face grabbed him as something desirable, hurtful and beyond his ability to reach.

"The door is unlocked," she said. "If you ain't here when I get off, make sure you leave my house the way I left it."

He was going to protest as he had the last time, that the furniture in the apartment was his, bought and paid for by him when he worked out in Argo. He objected to her suspicions of his untrustworthiness. He braced himself to point out that her skepticism of him was one of the reasons he'd left in the first place, but she overrode his attempt to speak.

"You can fix yo'self somethin' to eat. Babyjack ain't left for school yet. If he don't want to deal with you, don't push him. It might be better for all-a-us if you ain't here this evening." She looked at her watch and left the basement space. He was not fully awake. If he had not heard the uncertainty in her voice, he would have left that morning.

He slumped towards the ash tray, searching for a credible cigarette butt. Maybe he should keep going, head south again and find some less demanding, more needful woman. He hated sleeping on the pebbly couch out in the living room, while she slept sprawling and alone in the king-sized bed in the bedroom. He thought by now she would have allowed him to come to her to relieve himself inside of her instead of in his hand. The thought angered and repulsed him. How could he ever again touch her anger-filled body? He wanted to hit and fuck her at the same time.

He drove around the block two times, intrigued but unmoved by the plaintive purposes of people on the street. Three men dressed in ballooning work clothes stood around a hundred gallon drum passing a bottle, burning insulation from copper wires.

He wouldn't go into the row houses. He didn't know anyone down there. He cruised past the Seward Park field house and Cooley High School, which fronted Division Street and butted against the southbound Ravenswood El.

Jahdu, one of his old running buddies, waved him down in front of the Town & Garden apartments on Sedgwick St.

"Yo Holme! What you leanin' so low for, mane?" His expensive clothes smelled of cigarette smoke and alcohol.

"I'm lookin' for Baby. You seen 'im?"

He leaned into the car, partially concealing a bottle of pink Champale.

"What that l'il knucklehead chump done this time?"

"Hey man, you know."

"You runnin'?"

"Hey man this child drivin' me fuckin' crazy, Jim."

"Ya'll gon' do it? You been back 'bout a month now, right? You gon' stay wit' the bitch man?"

"Hey 'um back, ain't I?"

"That don't mean shit muthafucka. Yo ass been back befo' niggah." He looked both ways down the street and took a sip from his bottle.

"I gotta go man. I want to git this boy on in."

"C'mon and check out this good book 'um readin'."

He took a book of matches from his shirtpocket and flipped it open with his thumb. Between the red match tips, standing like the heads of an audience, he fingered a half-smoked joint and put it to his lips, striking the match in the book. Inhaling, Jahdu passed it to him through the darkened window.

Three hits and the world was softer, less pressing.

"Where you goin' now man?" Jahdu asked.

"I was gon' ride down North Avenue."

"I'll ride wit you a while. Ain't nothin' happenin' 'round here."

Jahdu got into the car and rolled another joint. Val drove around, listening to Jahdu and taking hits, until his reasons for everything grew less urgent. He stopped the car under the viaduct on Division Street near the J.W. Petersen Coal Company. Jahdu finished the Champale, opened the car door and gently set the bottle on the pavement.

"I wouldn't worry 'bout 'im man. He probably somewhere gettin' his l'il dick wet for the first time." They laughed, slapped palms. Jahdu grabbed his crotch and spat out of the window. Val closed his eyes. The car felt cocoon-like. Warm. Jahdu became his brother. He felt together they could endlessly defend themselves against whatever might come.

Two large women, one pregnant, dressed in makeshift domestic uniforms, got off of the Halsted Street bus and ambled slowly towards the projects. Val was surprised by the sudden darkness. Beneath an angle of concrete, the sky was indigo. He remembered the white pearls Lottie wore the night he first danced with her under blue lights at a set on the south side. She'd just finished her freshman year at Carbondale, tingling with the possibility of medical school. The luster of her teeth, the pearls, her angora sweater, the soft mound of her hips not moving away from him as he pressed closer, bolstered his certainty of his own worth and her affections.

After eighteen months of being without her, he'd come home to no home. He felt that he was living here for no other reason than habit, immune to the syphilitic spit of derelicts and the pigeon shit which fell to the windshield from unseen pigeons high overhead.

"This is mella!" Jahdu said. "Um 'spose to be startin' a new job Monday, man."

"Yeah?" Val said. "Where 'bout?"

"Motorola. I went out there with Perry Monday night and they called both of us yesterday. We went out there a coupla nights ago to see what time this gig is all about. We see these fuckin picture tubes comin' down this line. Hey man, that shit don't stop. I think we gon' work hard as ten muthafuckas on that line jim. And, oh yeah, when we get back outside we got a flat, right? No spare, right? Perry looks around the parkin' lot until he finds a car with his tire size and jack the muthafucka up and takes the man's tire. How did that fool ever get to be so crazy, man?"

"You ain't gon keep no job niggah," Val smiled, lighting a cigarette from Jahdu's pack.

"I gotta do somethin' man. I gotta git offa these streets. You know 'bout Miko don't you?"

"How his peoples dealin' with it?" Val asked.

"Hey, what they gon' do?"

Val rubbed his hands over his face as if he were washing it. He yawned.

"I saw yo brother Reggie a while back and I asked him where you went when you left home," Jahdu said.

"What did he say?"

"Said you took yo' sorry ass down south somewhere. Where'd you go man?"

"This l'il town in Alabama, just below Decatur, named Belle Mina."

"Yeah. What did you do down there man? Did you git a job?"

"Only work down there is temporary unless you know somebody or unless you move to Huntsville. I lived with this little girl and her mama. She had three kids and all of 'em had different daddies."

"So what was you doin, dealin' with the mama and the daughter?"

"Naw man. It's too deep to go into now. I gotta raise."

"Yo ho brutha man," Jahdu insisted. "Don't space on me that-a-way! So why did you hook up with this l'il deal man? Why did you go some ... how far is it down there man?" Val shrugged his shoulders. "Anyway, what did this l'il girl do for you that Lottie didn't, man?"

"She didn't want nothin' from me," Val said. "She didn't git into my business. Not a pressure-time thang, you know."

Val yawned and stretched, smelling his own sour breath bouncing off the windshield.

"I guess Baby at home now," he said, starting the engine.

"Drop me off in front of the Melody," Jahdu said. "Lavola probably there now."

He drove away as Jahdu swaggered up into a cluster of men standing in front of the Melody Lounge. The street lights had come on. He drove home and parked the car in front of the apartment building. A basketball game was in progress under the lights across the street. He felt tired now. The herb had mellowed him out. He did not want to rag Babyjack this time. He told himself that he would borrow Lottie Mae's portable T.V. and watch the baseball game tonight on the back porch.

Softly, he walked up the steps, thinking that tonight would be a good night to go to the Bel-Air Drive-in and see a double feature. He rubbed his hands together, thinking that he would suggest it in an insistent, yet considerate manner. He felt better, glad to be here. It was not home yet but he felt hopeful again.

He reached for his key at the second landing and remembered that Lottie asked him to give it back a few days ago. He whistled a piercing, incoherent melody as he ascended the steps. He wanted her to know that he had tried. Midway on the second landing he saw a piece of yellow legal paper taped to the door. He stomped up the steps and snatched it away. A layer of varnish remained on the Scotch tape.

"BABY BEEN SHOT. WE ARE AT HENROTIN."

All of the things he should have done in the last five years of his life rushed before him. They were crystal clear, as unmistakable as Lottie's displeasure. A great fear washed over him and he fought an uncontrollable chill, grasping the bannister, forcing himself to gather speed as he took two steps at a time going down. A door opened as he reached the second landing. Concerned faces peered out as if they had been waiting for this moment, to hear the violence in his footsteps in the hall. Their mouths were opened and moving, saying what he already knew. It was not until he was in the car fumbling with the keys, his fingers cold and shaking that he remembered he had to use the bathroom. He told himself he would sacrifice his need in the hope that getting there would make everything all right. What was the fastest way? For a moment he could not remember, could not think. Then he remembered. Up Wells Street, over to LaSalle. He got out of the car, leaving the motor running, the keys in the ignition, running now. Inside the emergency room, the night's wounded victims were strewn zombielike in orange and turquoise chairs. He asked the nurse where had they taken Babyjack.

"Are you the father?" she asked. She did not look up from her work. He nodded. He could not speak.

"Lorenzo Johnson is being operated on now. That's upstairs on the third floor."

When he got off of the elevator he saw two uniformed policemen and a detective standing over Lottie with clipboards and pencils moving. She was seated in a chair in the waiting area, her forehead in her hand. They all turned to face him as he went to her.

He sat next to her in a chair with irritating fabric. She looked at his eyes, turned her head slowly back to the policemen and continued to answer their questions.

The night nurse handed Val his keys when he left the hospital. An idling street cleaning vehicle took on water from a nearby hydrant. The driver of the vehicle squatted on the curb in back of the sweeper and leaned into the opened window of a police car, laughing.

It was four-thirty in the morning when Val parked under the el, across the street from the apartment. They sat in silence as the motor ticked, cooling down. He wished that she would say something. He wanted to tell her that he could change, he wanted to change. He knew the fabric of their life had been stretched, ripped, yet he wanted to ask her if he could stay. But deep down he knew this momentary feeling of responsibility was a sham.

"You shouldn't go in this morning," he said.

She turned to him, after staring for a time into the blackness beyond the windshield.

"Who gon' pay the bills then?" she snapped. She got out of the car and calmly shut the door. When she opened the door to the apartment building, he started the car and drove away.

The Man Who Loved Life

Simon Peter Dresser looked down at the long rows of tables. Pride made his heart grow in his chest, pressing against his throat so that he could hardly respond to the bishop sitting on his right. If only his daddy could see him now, bishops deferring to him, politicians courting him and hundreds of people looking up to where he sat at the center of the head table, admiration glowing from their faces.

His daddy had snorted when Simon told him he'd been asked to head the Illinois group. That was in 1975, two years after the baby murderers had persuaded the family haters on the Supreme Court to give women all over America abortion on demand.

Leave politics to the politicians, the old man had said. You got enough to do looking after your own family. Then he died before Simon's picture appeared in *Newsweek*. Died before Simon got the invitation to address the House of Bishops. He'd have seen that Simon truly was a rock, the rock on which a whole nation of Christians was building its hope of bringing morality back to America. Yes, Simon Peter, on this rock I will build my church. His daddy picked him to be the rock because he was the oldest and the younger ones had to obey him just like he had to obey his daddy. But sometimes the old man had his doubts. If only he could have lived to see this night.

Simon's heart started thudding faster and louder as he thought of the praise that lay ahead for him. Although the steak was cut thick and cooked the

way he liked it, just a little pink showing, he could
hardly taste it for excitement. But he politely handed
sour cream to the bishop and glanced at Louise to
make sure she was talking to the state representative
on her left. He'd tried to impress on her before they
left home how important it was to pay attention to
the man, how much Simon needed him to carry out
his program for Illinois, how she couldn't do her
usual trick of staring at her plate all through dinner.

When she saw him looking at her she flushed and
put down her fork and blurted something to her
dinner partner. Simon shook his head a little, but
nothing could really dampen his exultation. And it
wasn't fair to her, not really; she wasn't at home with
crowds and speeches as he was. She seldom came
with him to public events. She didn't like to leave the
children, even now that Tommy was eight and could
get along without her.

He turned back to the bishop and delivered a short
lecture on tactics in response to a comment the
prelate had made with the sour cream.

"Of course it's largely a social problem," the
bishop said when Simon finished. "The breakdown
of the family. Parents unwilling to assume any moral
authority. Very few with your kind of
family-centered life. But you don't need me to tell
you that."

"It's a question of respect," Simon said. "Children
don't respect their parents and their parents don't do
anything to force them to. It was different when you
and I were boys. You take my old man. You said
'yessir' when you spoke to him or he made sure you
never forgot a second time."

The bishop smiled in polite agreement and told a
long tale about the demoralized state of modern

seminary training. Simon took another roll and explained that his daddy had been tough. Tough, but fair. He'd sometimes felt hurt when he was little, but now he thanked God he had a father like that, one who knew right from wrong and wouldn't put up with any crap. Nossir, you thought you were being slick, putting one over the old man, but he was always a jump ahead of you. Had a hand as strong as a board. He wasn't afraid to use it, not even when you got to be big as him. Bigger.

The bishop nodded and shared an anecdote about the man he'd first served under as a priest.

Simon pursed his lips and shook his head at the right places. That time he'd gone out drinking with his buddies, he'd been eighteen, getting ready to start at St. Xavier's (stay with the Jesuits, his daddy said; they don't snivel every time some JD comes to them with a hard-luck story.) He'd thought he was old enough to do what he wanted on Saturday night.

Don't be a sissy, for Christ's sake. He was pretty sure it was Jimmy who had put it into words, Jimmy who was going into the army along with Bobby Lee Andrews. That was when being a soldier meant something, not like now, when all the soft liberals in Congress encouraged kids to burn their own country's flag. So he and Jimmy and Bobby went out with Carl and Joe. One last get-together for the team before they went their separate ways. The other guys were always on him, how he was scared of his old man. They didn't recognize it was respect, not fear. You respect the man who's strong enough to know right from wrong and teach it to you.

But just that one time he couldn't take their hassling any more. He got weak, soft, caved in and went out with them. And then two in the morning,

giggling drunk, trying to sneak in through the back
door. His mother had left the back door open. She
knew he was up to something so she snuck down
and unlocked it. She was always soft, always weak,
trying to subvert his daddy's strength. His father
made rules and she tried to break them, but she
couldn't. Nossir, not any more than her children. If
she was fifteen dollars shy in the grocery money his
daddy knew: he added all the bills against her
household allowance. Don't tell me you lost a
receipt, Marie, because I sure as hell don't believe
you. Where'd that money go to, anyway? And she'd
snuffle around and cry and try to lie, but his daddy
could always tell.

It was disgusting watching her cry; it made him
sick even to this day when he thought about it. He'd
told Louise that back the first year they were
married. Don't ever cry in front of your children, he
warned her. At least, I'd better not ever hear of you
doing it.

"The trouble is," he said to the bishop, "too many
men just are too lazy or too scared to buck all these
libbers and liberals and take on their role as head of
the family. They'd just as soon the government or the
schools or someone did it for them. That's why you
get all these girls going into the abortuaries and
letting someone murder their babies. Their daddies
or their husbands are just too damned—excuse me,
Your Grace—too darned lazy to control them."

The bishop smiled again, as if he was used to
hearing people swear and used to hearing them
apologize for it.

Simon's glow of satisfaction extended to his
well-run family. None of his five daughters ever
talked back to him. None of them had ever even

tried, except Sandra. She was the oldest; maybe she thought that gave her special status, but he'd sure as hell beaten that nonsense out of her.

He didn't believe it when she was born. When the nurse came out and told him it was a girl he knew she'd made a mistake, confused him with one of the other men waiting for news. His daddy'd been so disappointed. Disappointed but pleased at the same time: it proved he was a bigger man than Simon would ever be. Then it had taken three more tries before they got their first boy and he was a skinny little runt, took after Louise's family. And then his daddy died before they got their second boy. They named him Tom for his grandpa, and he looked like him, big, muscly boy, but it was too late; his daddy never saw Simon had finally gotten himself a real little man.

He realized he'd missed the bishop's next remark, but it didn't matter: he'd had the same conversation a hundred times and could respond without thinking. Not like the first time he'd talked to a bishop. Really talked, face to face, not just a handshake after a special service. He'd been so nervous his voice had come out in a little squeak, that high squeak he'd hated because it was how he always ended up sounding if he tried to argue with his daddy. But now he could see the bishops were men just like him, with the same kind of problems running their dioceses he had running his organization. Except now that he has head of the thing for the whole country it was probably more like being pope. Of course he never said any of this to the bishops, but it did give him a little edge over the man on his right. Just a suffragen, an assistant. Maybe twenty parishes under his care. Not like being responsible for the whole country.

The waitress filled Simon's coffee cup. He took cream and sugar from the bishop and used them generously. When he turned to offer them to Louise he saw she'd already been given some by the state representative. She shouldn't use so much sugar; she'd never really gotten her figure back after Tommy was born. But he wasn't going to spoil his big night by worrying about her problems.

As the bishop finished his dessert Simon's heart started its happy thudding once more. The bishop deliberately folded his napkin in threes across the diagonal and put it on the table so it was exactly parallel with his plate. He waited for the master of ceremonies to inform the diners that they would have grace after dinner, then slowly stood and offered the benediction.

Simon fixed a pleased but humble look under his beard. He leaned over to the bishop when he sat down and made a jovial little comment. The bishop nodded and chuckled and everyone on the floor could see that Simon was on equal, maybe even superior terms, with a bishop.

The master of ceremonies told everyone how happy he was they could be here to honor Simon. A staunch fighter for the unborn....Untold thousands of lives saved because of him....Wouldn't rest until babies were safe all over America....Special tribute tonight...But first they'd prepared a slide show: The Fight to Protect the Unborn.

The lights in the ballroom were dimmed and a screen unfolded on the stage behind the head table. Simon and the bishop turned their chairs around so they could see. After a second's hesitation, in which she looked first at Simon, then the state representative, Louise scooted around as well.

Simon had seen portions of the slide show before, sections that were used at fund-raising events and which showed him shaking hands with the President after their historic March for Life at the nation's capital. But they'd put that part together with a series taken at demonstrations and other important events around the country and added a soundtrack. The whole show had been completed in time for tonight's dinner. They'd use it in the future to educate high school students and church groups on how to fight for Life, but it was being unveiled tonight just for him.

Their logo flashed on the screen while solemn but cheerful music played behind it. The dove of the Holy Spirit spreading its wings over the curled form of a helpless fetus. Then his own voice, his well-practiced tenor that he'd spent four years in college studying speech to perfect, to get rid of that shameful squeak. It was a clip from the talk he'd made in Washington, the warm tones vibrating with emotion as he told the gathered hosts that no one in America could be free until every unborn life in America was held sacred.

While they played the speech, pictures flashed on the screen showing the mass of Pro-Life marchers carrying banners, holding up crosses to which they'd nailed cut-outs of murdered babies, all the marchers looking ardently at Simon, some with tears of shared passion in their eyes. Even now, six years later, listening to his own words his throat tightened again with rage felt on behalf of those million-and-a-half babies murdered every year. Hands as big as his father's coming down to choke the life out of them. Even when he'd been eighteen, old enough to go to college, he hadn't been big enough to stand up to the old man, so how could a poor helpless baby in the womb who didn't have any hands at all stand up for itself?

The show went on to display pictures of Pro-Life activists marching outside death camps. Cheers came from the audience when the photo of a fire-bombed death chamber was projected on the screen. They'd have to take that one out when they showed it to the high school students, but it proved that the helpless could gain power if they banded together.

The camera zoomed in close to the face of a girl going into one of the camps as she passed a line of peaceful picketers trying to get her to change her mind. Her face was soft, weak, scared.

Simon's fists clenched in his lap. Something about the girl made him think of his own mother. When his father beat him her face had that same expression, frightened but withdrawn, a bystander at the torment of her own baby. Don't do it, Thomas, she would beg, tears streaming down her face. He couldn't stand to hear her crying, as if she was the one being punished, and all the candy hearts she gave him later never really soothed him. He never let Louise cry. She'd done it the first time he'd had to give Sandra a whipping for talking back to him. She'd come to him sobbing as if being weak and scared was any way to stop him teaching his children right from wrong. He'd made it real clear she was never to do it again.

Then the girl in the picture was shown changing her mind. The Pro-Life counselor was able to persuade her to put Life above her own selfish desires to control her body. The audience cheered again as the girl walked off with the counselor to a Pro-Life clinic, funded with donations by tens of thousands of little people just like them who cared enough for Life to donate a few dollars every week.

Simon's fists relaxed and his mind wandered off to the remarks he'd make when his turn came. He'd worked on them all week, while flying to Toronto to protest the suspension of a policeman who wouldn't stand guard outside a death camp, while meeting in Springfield with key legislators on a number of bills to protect the unborn. He wanted to sound spontaneous, but authoritative, a leader people could rely on to make the right decisions.

Next to him Louise sucked in her breath, a little half-conscious sound of consternation. He glanced at her, then to the screen where she was staring. The picture showed a small band of picketers who faithfully came every Saturday to an abortuary in De Kalb. The soundtrack described how a few faithful could fight death and selfishness just as much as a big group could: the key was commitment. The Pro-Life counselor was exhorting a girl in a lime-green parka as she headed up the path to the death chamber entrance.

Each shot moved in closer to the head bent in fear and weakness. Simon knew this face without seeing, knew it by the color of the parka, by the way the fine brown hair parted over the bowed white neck. His bowels were softening and turning over and his throat was so dry he could only trust himself to whisper.

"You did this," he hissed to Louise under the flow of the soundtrack. She shook her head dumbly. "You knew about this. You knew about this and never told me." She only shook her head again, her eyes filling with tears. She turned to grab her napkin, turned so fast that she jarred the table and knocked a glass of water down the state representative's back.

The accident made her throat work with suppressed hysteria as she tried wiping her face, then the legislator's back. The state representative was gracious, helping to mop the front of her dress, laughing off the damp patch on his back, but Simon was sure he would be chuckling about him with other colleagues before the week was over: why should we listen to Simon? He can't even control his own wife.

Simon grabbed Louise's left arm and pulled her head down close to his mouth. "You go off to the ladies' room," he ordered in that same voiceless hiss. "You leave now and don't come back until I'm through with my speech, you hear?"

Dumbly she pulled her arm away, apologizing through her tears to the state representative, dropping her handbag, spilling lipstick and Kleenex on the man's lap. The legislator patted her on the shoulder, tried to make out that he didn't mind, that it was an accident and he didn't need her to dry his back or pay to have his suit cleaned. She gave the man a fixed little smile and stumbled from the stage. If she'd practiced for a month she couldn't have done more to humiliate him.

The bishop leaned over and asked with unctuous concern if Louise was all right. Simon managed a twisted smile.

"She's fine. Just needs to go to the ladies'."

But he could kill her for this. Kill her for destroying him at his moment of triumph, for working hand in glove with the old man to get him. He really thought he'd die. That night he came home drunk from being out with his buddies and his daddy stood waiting by the refrigerator with a baseball bat.

You tell me one reason why I shouldn't use this on you, Simon Peter. The rock. The old man spat at him. The sand. I'm like a man who built his house on the sand. And Simon tried talking to him, tried making his voice come out big and booming to say he was a man, he could go out with his buddies if he wanted, but the only thing that came out was that terrible little squeak and then the old man was hitting him, hitting him so hard he ended up on the floor, peeing in his pants. He was lying on the floor all wet and bleeding and sobbing while his mother stood crying at the top of the stairs, her tiny voice pleading for him.

And all the while Sandra's silhouette mocked him from the screen. "One of our failures," the soundtrack intoned. "We didn't have the resources to give this girl the help she needed to choose Life. But with your support we'll be able to help other girls like this one, so that truly every life in this great land of ours will be held sacred."

Tony Ardizzone

Idling

Sometimes when I'm hauling I drive right past her house. The Central Avenue exit from the Kennedy Expressway, and then north maybe two, three miles. The front is red brick and the awnings are striped, like most of the other houses on Central Avenue. Her name was Suzy and she was the kind of girl who liked cheese and sauerkraut on her hot dogs. She was regular. She went in for plain skirts, browns and navy blues, wrap-arounds, and those button-down blouses with the tiny pinstripes all the girls wore back then. She must be as old as I am now, and the only girl ever to wear my ring. She was special. Suzy was my only girl.

I met her at a party at a friend's house. A Saturday night, and I was on the team, only I had pulled my back a couple of days before—too serious to risk playing, they said, sorry, we think you're out for the season. I'd been doing isometrics. And though they gave me the chance to dress and sit with the team I said the hell with it, this season's finished, get somebody else to benchwarm with the sophomores.

Which was O.K., because the night I met Suzy the team was playing out in Oak Park, and had I gone I'd have met my father afterwards for some pizza, like we usually did after a game, but instead I went over to Ronny's. The two of us hung around the back of his garage, talking, splitting a couple of six-packs, with him soaking out a carburetor and me trying to figure if what I had done with the team was right. Ronny told me stuff it, you can't play you can't

play. There are things nobody can control, he said.
You just got to learn to roll with the punches. He
was maybe my best friend back then and I was
feeling lousy—here it was not even October and only
the second game. Let's get drunk, Ronny said,
laughing, so I said stuff it too, there's a party out in
Des Plaines tonight. So we got in his car and drove
there. Then some of the game crowd got there, all
noisy and excited, and I met Suzy.

It went real smooth and I should have known
then, like when you're beating your man easy on the
first couple of plays you should know if you've got
any sense that he's gonna try something on you on
the third. I started talking to her, thinking that since
I was a little drunk I had an excuse if she shut me
down—maybe I even wanted to be shut down, I
don't know, I was still feeling lousy—but she talked
back and we danced some. Slow dances, on account
of my back. And when I told her my name she said
you're on the team, I saw you play last week. I said
yeah, I was. She seemed impressed by that. But she
didn't remember that it was me who intercepted that
screen pass in the third quarter, and damn I nearly
scored. She smiled, and I held her.

Things went real fine then. We danced a lot, and
later Ronny flipped me his keys, and me and Suzy
went out for a ride. Mostly we talked, her about that
night's game, and me about why I'd decided not to
suit up, which, I told her, was really the best thing
for me. There's something stupid about dressing and
not playing. If they win, sure it's your victory too,
but what did you do to deserve it? And if they lose
you feel just as miserable.

I took her home then and told her I wanted to see her again, and all the talking made me sober up, and that started it.

I don't know if you've ever had duck's blood soup. It's a Polish dish, and honest to God it's made with real duck's blood, sweet and thick, and raisins and currants and noodles. Her father, the father of three beautiful little girls, with Suzy the oldest, took us all out to this restaurant on North McCormick Street and he ordered it for me. He said the name in Polish to the waiter, then looked at me and winked. He even bought me a beer, and I was only seventeen. The girls watched me as I salted it and kept asking me how it tasted. I didn't understand. I said it tasted sweet. Then Suzy's mother laughed out loud at me and told me what was in it. I think she wanted me to be surprised.

Suzy went out with me for her image. There was no other reason, it was as simple as that. Now there's no glory in dating a former defensive end. Suzy went out with me because the year before I had dated Laurie Foster, and Laurie Foster had a reputation at Saint Scholastica, where Suzy went to school. This is where everything gets crazy. Laurie somehow had a reputation, which I don't think she deserved, at least not when I was taking her out. We never did much really of anything, but because I had dated her I got a reputation too, and I never even knew about it. I guess there was some crazy kind of glory in dating and going steady with a guy who had a rep.

She said let me wear your ring, hey, just for tonight, and I said sure, Suzy. And she asked me if I liked her and I said of course, don't you like me? She laughed and said no, I'm just dating you for your looks. I was a little drunk that night and she said do you ever think about it, Mike, do you ever just sit down and think about it, and I said what, and she said going steady. I told her no. Then she asked me if I wanted to date other girls, and when I said no I didn't she said well, I think we should then, and finally I said it's all right with me, Suzy, if you think it's that important, and she said it is, Mike, it really is. She wore my ring on a chain around her neck until she got a size adjuster, then she wore my ring on her hand.

Pretty much of everything we did then was her idea, not that I didn't have some ideas of my own. But Suzy initiated pretty much of everything for a while back then. Ronny was dating a girl who lived near Suzy out on Touhy Avenue, and I remember once when we were double-dating Suzy and I were in the back seat of the car fooling around and she said can't you unclasp it, and I said oh, sure. And that time we were studying at the table in her kitchen—her mother was down in the basement ironing, and her father was still at work—and she says not here, Mike, but hey maybe in the front room.

She said hold me honey, hey, and she touched me and I touched her and she was wet and smelled like strawberries and her mouth nipped my neck as I held her. She said Mike, do you like me I mean really do you like me, and I said yes, Suzy, that's a crazy question I really like you, and she held me and made me stop and we sat up when we heard her mother coming up from the basement.

The next weekend I bought some Trojans, and Ronny lent me his car for the night. But before I went to pick her up the two of us got a little drunk in his garage. Ronny said I'd better try one first to make sure they weren't defective. He said people in those places prick them with pins all the time just for laughs, and I said yeah, I sure hope this thing'll hold, and Ronny said there's seventeen years of it built up inside of you, remember, and I said damn, maybe she'll explode, and he said she'd better not on my upholstery, and we laughed and he threw a punch at me and we drank another beer and then blew one up and it held good and we let it fly outside in the alley.

The back seat was cold and cramped, and Suzy cried when it was over, and we wiped up the blood with a rag. It meant something, I thought, and I started taking going steady a little more serious after that.

It must have been the next month that her mother started in on me. She was young then and still very pretty for a woman who'd had three kids, and she began out of nowhere saying little things like here, Mike, take a chair, and did you really hurt your back or is there some other reason why you quit the team? I had always tried to be polite to her. Then Suzy started to get on me, asking me sometimes exactly what was I doing when I pulled my back, how was I standing, and couldn't I maybe try out for track or baseball or something in the spring? I couldn't figure where they were coming from, and I tried to explain that even before I got hurt I hadn't been that good of a football player, that I'd been on the team simply because I'd liked to run and play catch with my father on fall afternoons. Suzy's father seemed to understand, and he'd tell me stories about his old high school team, funny stories about crazy plays and the stuff the players wore that was supposed to be their equipment, and then sometimes he'd get serious and say it wasn't a sport anymore at all now, that it was a real butcher shop, a game for the biggest sides of beef, and if he had a son he'd let the boy play if he wanted to but he'd hope his kid would have the good sense to know when to quit. Because all athletes have to quit sooner or later, he said. Everyone quits everything sooner or later. The trick is knowing how and when. Toward the end I got to know him a little. I'd go over there sometimes even when I didn't feel like seeing Suzy but when I knew there was a game or something else good on TV, and once the three of them came over to my house in the city and the three of us, me and my father and Suzy's father, sat around and shot the breeze and had ourselves a good time, and we must have drunk a whole case of beer, and Suzy and her mother ended up out by themselves talking in the kitchen.

Suzy's father asked me how I quit the team, and told me once he had worked for a guy and after a while he realized he was getting nowhere. He said even though they already had Suzy and needed every penny they could get, one day he sat down with his boss and told him that he simply couldn't work there any longer. He said Mike, there are things sometimes that you just have to do, but you need to learn that it's almost as important to go about doing them in a decent way. I told him that maybe I had been a little hotheaded with the coaches. He said he respected me for what I did, on account of it showed that things mattered to me, but maybe staying on the team and picking up a few splinters on the sidelines might have been a better way to go about doing it.

I knew even back then that me and Suzy weren't going to last long, and then I started realizing that what we were doing was serious business, especially if Suzy got pregnant. I was cool towards her then. It

was around this time that I found out from the guys
at school that she had gone out on the sly with
another guy. This guy, she told me when I asked her
about it, was her second cousin who was having
some temporary trouble finding himself a date. I
laughed good at that and said damn it, at least if you
would've told me I wouldn't have had to hear it from
the guys, and we both found out then that I really
didn't much care. We had a long talk then, and then
for a while things went O.K.

For a while. Until May, until I was walking down
the second-floor corridor at school and I got wind
from Larry Souza, a guy who was dating one of
Suzy's friends, about a surprise six months'
happy-going-steady party Suzy was going to throw
for me, with all the girls from Scholastica and the
guys from Saint George invited too and even some
kind of a cake, with MIKE & SUZY in bright red
icing written on the top, and me and Ronny were
sitting in his garage late one night drinking some
beer and talking, and then we were thinking
wouldn't it be something if I didn't show, wouldn't
that be a real kicker, and then the night of the big
party comes along, with me expected to drop by at
around nine, just another date, Mike, maybe we'll
stay home, sit around and watch a movie on TV or
maybe if the folks aren't home we can sneak
downstairs after the little ones go to bed and you
know what, and at eight me and Ronny are in his
garage scraping spark plugs and still talking about it
and laughing, and at eight-thirty we need just a drop
more of beer so we drive out, and by nine we're
stopping by the lake because Ronny thinks he sees an
old girlfriend racing down Pratt Street on her bicycle
and I'm saying damn, Ronny, that girl must be

thirty-five years old but we drive there anyway and
end up sitting on the trunk of his old Chevy sharing
another six-pack, still laughing, and then we meet
some kids who've got a football and Jesus it's a
beautiful night, a gorgeous night in May, and we
pick sides and then some girls come along and we
ask if they want to play, it's only touch, and below
the waist and not in the front, honest, and we've got
some beer left in the car if you're thirsty first hey
come on, and I'm guarding this goon who couldn't
even tie his own shoes by himself let alone run in a
straight line and on the very first play Ronny is
throwing to him high and hard and the clown falls
down and I move up and over him and make the
interception, easy, and I'm laughing so hard I stop
right where I catch it and let the boob tag me, here,
tag me, I'm going nowhere, I'll tag myself, hey
everybody please tag me, laughing so hard and we
play until past eleven when a police Park Control car
comes crunching up the cinder track and this big cop
gets out and says all right kids, the park is closed,
and one of the girls says please officer please, have a
heart, why don't you take off your gun and stick
around and play, and the big cop says sorry, wish to
Christ I could, and we all laugh at that, and then
Ronny and I say hey who wants to go for a ride and
two of the girls say sure, where, and Ronny looks at
me and shrugs and I say damn, anywhere is O.K. by
me, so we all get in and we drive and drive and drive,
nearly all the way up to Wisconsin, the four of us
drinking what beer is left and stopping here and
there along the road to see if we can buy some more,
I'm sorry, come back in three years, they say, and I'm
telling this girl who looks like the Statue of Liberty
holding up her cigarette the way girls do in the dark

car with the tip of it all glowing all about what I did that night, and she says can you picture them all waiting and then you don't show, surprise, and then we have ourselves a contest to see who can guess what kind of cake it was and Ronny says chocolate and his girl guesses pineapple but my girl comes up with angel food and we laugh and say she wins, I give her her prize, a kiss, and damn she kisses back, hard, and then Ronny stops on this quiet road in the middle of the blackness and says hey, where do you want to go now, and I say Canada, and my girl says take a left, and Ronny turns and says what's left, and his girl says we're left and I want to stay right here, and damn that is funny and we drive and drive and drive, and it's long past three and silent like a church when I finally get to my house.

My dad is awake and angry, worried that I'd been in an accident. They called here four times, Mike, he says, and what can I tell them I don't even know where my own son is. When I tell him what happened he says that was a downright shitty thing to do, then he shakes his head and says what would your mother have thought? I think of Suzy's father, how I never thought that he might have been worried, and my father says you should call them right now and apologize. I say it's late, too late to bother them, and he says you're old enough now to think for yourself, do what you do, I'm going to bed.

I didn't call there for a couple of days and by then Suzy had found out what happened. The first thing she said was when can you pick up your ring? I said hey Suzy, I don't want you to give me my ring back, and she said that ring must've cost you forty dollars, and we start to argue.

Her youngest sister answered the door, looking like Suzy must have when she was that young, and you know I bet like her mother too, clean-faced, eyes all shining, with freckles across the bridge of her nose. She tells me to come in. I try to smile to make her smile, but then her father comes down the stairs coughing into a handkerchief and holding my ring in an envelope. I tried to talk to him, to explain, but I didn't know what to say.

Now I drive for Cook County. A GMC truck and mostly light construction materials for building projects. It's not a bad job. A year or so after I finished high school Suzy's mother died, some kind of crazy disease that I guess she knew all about before but didn't tell anyone about, and when I heard I drove out to the house. Her father came to the door and told me Suzy was out. I said I came to see you. He nodded then, looking at me. Then instead of inviting me in he told me that he was busy packing to move to his sister's out East, and then he said he'd tell Suzy I stopped by and that I should be sure to thank my father for the sympathy card he'd sent.

When we'd kiss she'd close her eyes and keep them closed, tight, and I'd look at her sometimes in the back seat of Ronny's old Chevy going up the street with the bands of light moving across her face. And once when we were at the lake she took my hand and said Mike, do you ever just think about it? I asked what, and she said oh nothing, Mike, I guess I just mean about things.

The coaches hollered at me after that interception, like I was a damn rookie sophomore. They said I caught the ball and stood still. But they were wrong—as sure as I know my own name I know I ran. My body moved up and toward the ball, it struck my hands and then my numbers, I squeezed it and went for the goal line. I think about that sometimes when I'm hauling, and sometimes I pull over on Central Avenue and look at the red bricks and striped awnings. I think of Suzy and her father. I grip the truck's wheel, my engine idling.

Contributors' Notes

TONY ARDIZZONE was born and raised on Chicago's North Side and was graduated from the University of Illinois in 1971. He is the author of two novels, *In the Name of the Father* and *Heart of the Order*, as well as a collection of short stories, *The Evening News*, which received the 1985 Flannery O'Connor Award for Short Fiction. His work has also been awarded the Virginia Prize for Fiction, the Lawrence Foundation Award, and two fellowships from the National Endowment for the Arts. He has just completed work on *Larabi's Ox*, an interconnected book of stories set in Morocco. He lives in Bloomington, Indiana, where he teaches in the creative writing program at Indiana University.

GEORGE BAILEY was born in Madison County, Alabama, in 1946. He received his B.A. in Creative Writing from Columbia College and his M.A. in English from DePaul University. He teaches composition, literature, and public speaking in the English department at Columbia College. His short fiction and articles on a variety of topics have appeared in the *Chicago Sun-Times*, *Fra Noi*, and *Exchange* magazine. He is currently working on a novel and a collection of short stories. The editor of the forthcoming anthology *West Side Stories*, he lives in Chicago with his wife Linda and their two sons.

STEVE BOSAK's novel *Gammon* was published in 1985 by St. Martin's. He earned an M.F.A. in Writing from the University of Arkansas and teaches in the English department at Columbia College, where he directs the Professional Writing Program. He is a native of Chicago's south side, where he currently lives. A frequent contributor to literary journals and computer magazines, he is the editor of the forthcoming anthology *South Side Stories*.

ANA CASTILLO is a poet, novelist, editor, and translator. Her work is widely anthologized in the U.S., Mexico, and Europe. She writes in both English and Spanish, and her work has been translated into German and Bengali. She is the author of four collections of poetry: *Women Are Not Roses*

(University of Houston/Arte Publico, 1984); *My Father Was A Toltec* (West End, 1988) and two poetry chapbooks, *The Invitation* and *Otro Canto*. Her first novel, *The Mixquiahuala Letters* (Bilingual Review Press, 1986) won the Before Columbus Foundation's American Book Award. Her latest novel, *Sapagonia* (Bilingual Review Press, 1990), was nominated for a Western States Book Award. She co-edited and co-translated the Spanish adaptation of the well known feminist anthology *This Bridge Called My Back*. She is a recipient of a California Artists Fellowship in fiction (1989) and a National Endowment for the Arts Fellowship in poetry (1990). Currently she is at work on *Massacre of the Dreamers: Mexican-Indian Women in the U.S. 500 Years after the Conquest* for her doctoral dissertation at the University of Bremen.

MAXINE CHERNOFF's poems and stories have appeared in numerous publications, including *Story, Mississippi Review, The Paris Review, New Directions, Partisan Review, Iowa Review, Playgirl, Triquarterly*, and *Formations*. A native Chicagoan, she is the author of five books of poems, one of which, *New Faces of 1952*, won the 1985 Carl Sandburg Award for poetry. Her book of stories *Bop* (Vintage Contemporaries) received an award from Friends of American Writers and the LSU/*Southern Review* Short Fiction Award for 1988. The *NYTBR* said, "Maxine Chernoff has an eye for detail that is simultaneously sharp and compassionate. *BOP* is generous with its moments of recognition and pleasure." She teaches in the City Colleges of Chicago (Truman College) and is a visiting lecturer in creative writing at the School of the Art Institute of Chicago. A winner of five Illinois Arts Council Literary Fellowships and a PEN Syndicated Fiction Award, she received her M.A. at the University of Illinois, Chicago. She is a Fellow at Simon's Rock of Bard College. Along with Paul Hoover, she co-edits the award-winning magazine *New American Writing*.

Of her newest collection, *Leap Year Day: New and Selected Poems*, Andrei Codrescu said, "If the world could look through Maxine's eye for even five minutes every day, there would be no need whatsoever for the pompous self-righteousness that currently spoils the *polis*. Her views of human life are wise and instructive tales that cure by correcting perspective. She is one of our best *zaddiks*. It's the truth." Her novel *Plain Grief* will be published in spring 1991 by Simon and Schuster.

FRED L. GARDAPHÈ, a native Chicagoan, is professor of English at Columbia College in Chicago where he teaches "Chicago in Literature" among other literature and composition courses. His play, "Vinegar and Oil," was produced in Chicago in 1987 by the Italian American Theatre Company. He has published short fiction, critical essays, and reviews in journals, newspapers and books. He is contributing editor of *Italian American Ways*. He is co-editor, with Anthony Tamburri and Paul Giordano, of *From the Margin: Writings in Italian Americana*. He is also co-founder, with Tamburri and Giordano, and review editor of the journal *VIA: Voices in Italian Americana*. He is currently completing his Ph.D. in American Literature at the University of Illinois at Chicago.

PAUL HOOVER's novel *Saigon, Illinois* was published by Vintage Contemporaries in 1988. "Demonstration," a chapter of that book, first appeared in *The New Yorker*. He is also the author of *The Novel*, a long poem recently published by *New Directions*, as well as several other books of poetry: *Letter to Einstein Beginning Dear Albert, Somebody Talks a Lot, Nervous Songs,* and *Idea*. His work has appeared in *Paris Review* and *Partisan Review*. A recipient of the GE Award for Younger Writers in 1984 and the Carl Sandburg Award for Poetry in 1987, he has lived in Chicago since 1968, when he left Indiana to begin his alternative service as a conscientious objector to the Vietnam War. The winner of two Illinois Arts Council Literary fellowships, he co-edits *New American Writing* and directs the Poetry Program at Columbia College.

SUSAN LYNNE HOUSE, a native of Delaware, came to Chicago in the early 1970's after the security police at Washington, D.C.'s National Airport mistook the wind-up alarm clock in her backpack for a bomb and ordered her to leave. The next plane was going to Chicago. Having been mistaken for a revolutionary, she decided to stay and fight for women's rights by liberating the Welfare Rehabilitation Center's welding school. For the next decade and a half she worked as a welder and union activist while attending local colleges, completing a B.A. in English at Mundelein's Weekend College. Today she lives on the north side, serves on the Board of the Chicago Consortium for Worker Education and teaches in a program she founded for the union at the Stewart Warner plant where she used to work. Her work has appeared in *Tradeswoman* magazine and in *Mundelein Review*.

ANGELA JACKSON was born in Greenville, Mississippi, but moved to Chicago at an early age. The fifth of nine children, she lived on the south side in the same house until she left for college. Educated at Northwestern and the University of Chicago, she credits the community-based OBAC (Organization of Black American Culture) Writers Workshop under Hoyt W. Fuller with her early development as a writer. Other credit she gives to her mother, who was an avid reader, and a father who was an accomplished storyteller and amateur blues lyricist. Jackson has published poetry and fiction in a number of journals, including *Black World, NOMMO, Essence, Yellow Silk, Black American Literature Forum, Triquarterly, StoryQuarterly, Chicago Review*, and *Callaloo*. The best of her several collections of poetry will appear in *And All These Roads Be Luminous* (Third World Press, 1991). *Treemont Stone*, a novel from which "The Blue Rose" is excerpted, is the first of a trilogy. Jackson is the winner of numerous awards, including the Pushcart Prize for Poetry, 1989; NEA and Illinois Arts Council (IAC) Fellowships in 1979 and 1980; IAC Literary Awards for Fiction, and the Hoyt W. Fuller Award for Literary Excellence from the DuSable Museum.

TOM JOHNSON is a labor writer and teacher who lives on Chicago's northwest side with his wife, Rosemary Armocida, an early childhood educator, and their seven year-old daughter, Theresa Anne. Johnson's grandparents emigrated from Italy and Sweden to the Chicago neighborhoods of Portage Park and Brighton Park. His poetry, fiction, and journalism have won local and national awards, including the Max Steinbock Award (1989) from the International Labor Communications Association. Johnson's work also appears in the anthology *Writing About Work by the People Who Do It* (1988, RoughCut).

Born in 1941, **THOMAS J. KEEVERS** has lived in Chicago all of his life. He spent ten years with the Chicago Police Department, five of them as a homicide detective. Currently he is a trial lawyer practicing in Chicago. His fiction has appeared in *Chicago Literary Review*, *The Clothesline Review*, and *Wind*.

KAREN LEE OSBORNE was born in Washington, D.C. and grew up in Florida, the setting for her novel *Carlyle Simpson* (Academy Chicago, 1986). Widely praised by the critics, *Carlyle Simpson* won both the First Prize from Friends of American Writers and the Chicago Foundation for Literature Award. The *Chicago Tribune* called it "one of the best novels of this year." She earned her M.A. and Ph.D. in English at the University of Denver. During 1985–86 she was a Fulbright lecturer on American literature in the Soviet Union. Her work has appeared in numerous publications, including *The Denver Quarterly*, *The Literary Review*, *Women's Review of Books*, *Conditions*, *Sojourner*, *Nit & Wit*, *Other Voices*, and *Sing Heavenly Muse*. A resident of Chicago since 1986, she is a contributor to *Naming the Daytime Moon: Stories and Poems by Chicago Women*. Her second novel, *Hawkwings*, will be published in spring 1991 by Third Side Press. A collection of stories, *Sunshine Skyway*, is also forthcoming. She teaches in the English department at Columbia College.

SARA PARETSKY was born in 1947, grew up in Kansas, and moved to Chicago in 1968. She earned her Ph.D. in history at the University of Chicago and worked for nine years as a manager with a multinational finance company. Her series of bestselling V.I. Warshawski novels include

Killing Orders, Indemnity Only, Deadlock, Bitter Medicine, Blood Shot, and *Burn Marks.* She was named Woman of the Year by *Ms. Magazine* in 1988. She is the recipient of the Friends of American Writers Award for *Deadlock* and won the Silver Dagger Award from the British Crimewriters Association for *Blood Shot.* She co-founded the organization Sisters in Crime for women writers. A frequent contributor to national journals, she lives in Hyde Park on Chicago's south side.

FORTHCOMING TITLES from CITY STOOP

West Side Stories

edited by George Bailey

featuring Aaron Freeman, Bill Campbell, Diane Williams, and many others

Publication date: July 1991
Prepublication price (including shipping): $7.95
ISBN 0-9627425-1-1

coming in winter/spring 1992
South Side Stories
edited by Steve Bosak

Yes, I want to order _____ copies of *West Side Stories* at $7.95 each.

Ship to:

_____

_____

_____

Amount enclosed: _____
Make checks payable to **City Stoop Press**.
Order from:
City Stoop Press
4317 N. Wolcott
Chicago, IL 60613